'Ah, so you [...] **expert on wo** [...]

'I like to think so. For instance, I can usually tell what women are thinking when I'm with them.'

'And what am I thinking now?' she asked facetiously, turning her face to look into his eyes, which were dangerously close to hers.

'You're thinking about what you'll do when Matthew falls asleep. Trying to decide whether you'll persuade me to drive you home or whether you'll simply enjoy the rest of the evening with me.'

'Partially true,' she said, still maintaining the light tone.

'Well, it looks like our little cherub is well satisfied now, so why don't you put him down in the cot and let me help you come to the right decision?'

Our little cherub—not *your* little cherub, Carlos had said. A slip of the tongue, perhaps, but it affected her deeply. It was as if the three of them had formed a family unit...or was she being impossibly romantic?

As a full-time writer, mother and grandmother, **Margaret Barker** says: 'I feel blessed with my lifestyle, which has evolved over the years and included working as a State Registered Nurse. My husband and I live in a sixteenth-century thatched house near the East Anglian Coast. We are still very much in love, which helps when I am describing the romantic feelings of my heroines. In fact, if I find the creative flow diminishing, my husband will often suggest we put in some more research into the romantic aspects that are eluding me at the time!'

Recent titles by the same author:

THE GREEK SURGEON
A CHRISTMAS TO REMEMBER
THE PREGNANT DOCTOR

THE SPANISH DOCTOR

BY
MARGARET BARKER

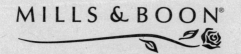

MILLS & BOON®

First published in Great Britain 2002
Harlequin Mills & Boon Limited,
Eton House, 18-24 Paradise Road, Richmond, Surrey TW9 1SR

© Margaret Barker 2002

ISBN 0 263 83083 7

Set in Times Roman 10½ on 12 pt.
03-0802-46991

Printed and bound in Spain
by Litografia Rosés, S.A., Barcelona

CHAPTER ONE

THESE airline seats were far too close for people with long legs! Pippa shifted her bottom as much as was possible in the cramped conditions, but the backache was still there. Not surprising she was suffering some discomfort, really.

She'd been on the go since the crack of sparrows, and, at thirty-six weeks pregnant, she really should have tried to find somewhere to put her feet up for a few minutes before getting on the flight. But in the crowded waiting lounge at the airport it had seemed impossible and she'd been trying not to draw too much attention to her condition.

'Everything all right?' The air stewardess gave Pippa a reassuring smile as she paused in the aisle.

'Fine!' Pippa returned the smile, determined not to admit, even to herself, that she was having awful suspicions about what was happening to her.

The stewardess passed further down the plane but Pippa knew she was keeping an eye on her. All the cabin staff would have been alerted to the fact that the pregnant woman in the aisle seat on row twenty-eight was only four weeks from full term. Normally the airline would have been reluctant to let her fly, but Pippa's London obstetrician had given her the required papers saying she was fit to fly.

The last thing James had said to her after he'd examined her yesterday had been, 'Now, don't let me down, will you? It's little more than a two-hour flight, so I'm sure you'll be OK. You're an extremely fit young woman and you've sailed through this pregnancy so far. There's absolutely no reason why you shouldn't stay that way for another four weeks. And anyway, an experienced midwifery-trained staff nurse like you would recognise any untoward symptoms and cancel the flight yourself, wouldn't you?'

She'd given James a confident, 'Of course.'

But that had been yesterday. Today was different. Ian's call from the States in the early hours of the morning had not only disrupted her sleep but had made it impossible for her to stop worrying for the rest of the night. As she'd dragged herself out of bed she'd felt awful, and during her early-morning shower it had been difficult to ignore the dragging feeling low down in her abdomen.

Her baby was definitely not as high up in the womb as he'd been yesterday. He'd decided to move downwards in the night, but this was normal during the last few weeks of pregnancy...except it did feel as if his head was well-aimed at the birth canal, as if preparing to swoop lower still and make his way into the world.

If she hadn't been midwifery trained she probably wouldn't have picked up on it. She'd have put it all down to missing her sleep and would just have thought it was normal to find it harder to move around in her elephantine waddle. And there had been no other symptoms until she'd got to the airport so she hadn't felt she was putting either herself or her precious baby at risk. It had been when she was sitting in the airport lounge, trying not to be too impatient with the two-hour delay, that the backache had started.

If only the plane hadn't been delayed, she would have been almost there!

But, as she kept telling herself, it was only a short flight to Spain. Unlike the long journeys which she and her brother used to endure as children, sitting in the back of the family car seemingly for days on end before they'd reached the Spanish campsite where they'd always spent their summer holidays.

So, if she really was going into the first stage of labour, there was still plenty of time. Most of the babies she'd delivered to first-time mums had taken their time. But there had been one or two clever little mites who'd speeded things up and taken everybody by surprise.

Oh, please, don't let me have one of those inside me! Unconsciously, she put a hand over her bump in a protective gesture. Already she loved this baby dearly. If it was possible to bond with a foetus she'd already done that. When the weird mists on the ultrasound scan had evolved into the image of a darling little baby boy, she'd immediately given him a name. Her baby had been Matthew for weeks now, and she couldn't wait to hold him in her arms.

It didn't make any difference to her that Matthew's father was a two-timing, scheming, not-to-be-trusted charmer. She'd been in love with Ian when Matthew had been conceived, and that was the thought she must dwell on if ever she found herself becoming impatient with her little boy. The sins of the father had nothing to do with her precious son.

The man sitting next to her turned and gave her a worried look. Pippa realised she hadn't actually spoken but she'd certainly made some kind of sound. Had she moaned or done anything embarrassing? Her head was feeling a bit light and fuzzy now and she couldn't remember.

The man next to her leaned forward. 'Are you all right?'

'Yes, I'm fine!' she said quickly.

She realised immediately that her tone had been decidedly brusque. But she'd had enough of the well-meaning but curious passengers during the long airport wait, who'd wanted to know where her husband was. Wasn't she brave to be travelling on her own when she was so obviously nearing her time? How long was it before the baby was due, exactly? Was it her first?

Her fellow passenger gave her a puzzled look as if to say there had been no need to bite his head off.

'I'm sorry if I sounded ungrateful for your concern, but I'm just a bit tired, that's all. It's been a long day and I need to get some rest.'

As she closed her eyes Pippa realised that she'd probably made things worse. The man had only been trying to help, and now the atmosphere was decidedly cool. Well, she certainly wasn't in the mood for conversation. She had to concentrate on remaining calm and relaxed. Anyway, the man next to her had a distinct Spanish accent so he might not speak much English. Yes, from what she'd noticed, he had that rugged Mediterranean look, dark tanned skin, deep brown eyes, black hair…

Actually, she'd taken in quite a lot about him. Did it mean she wasn't entirely immune to appraising men? Well, that was a good sign that her pregnancy hadn't completely removed her femininity! She was looking forward to shedding her load and wearing decent clothes again, wearing strappy sandals and be-ing able to run for a bus…

She opened her eyes and turned her head slightly. She'd been right about his nationality. He was reading a Spanish newspaper now, ignoring her completely.

Good! She didn't want to bring attention to herself. She thought about how she'd tried to ignore the dis-comfort in her abdomen as she'd waited in the airport lounge. She'd told herself it must be the lack of sleep, and maybe the prawn curry she'd eaten the night be-fore. For the last few weeks she'd been hooked on prawn curry but sometimes it wasn't too good for her digestion. It was nothing to do with the baby. It was merely a twinge, a—

'Ooh!'

This time she really had vocalised her feelings, as the backache had turned into a grinding pain that took away all her doubts about her condition. It was no use pretending any longer. She was definitely going into labour. And they were barely thirty minutes into the flight! This was a definite contraction she was experiencing.

The Spanish man had looked up from his paper enquiringly but hadn't spoken to her. Probably re-specting her obvious desire for privacy, he was taking care not to get his head bitten off again, Pippa thought as she clung to the sides of her seat. She ought to try to relax, but advising patients what to do and putting things into practice were quite separate at the mo-ment.

The pain was easing. She would go to the loo and sort herself out, see if she could gauge how things were going and form some kind of strategy to cope with the situation. It should be possible to hold on for the remaining part of the journey, and then she could check herself into the hospital in plenty of time for the actual birth.

Her friend Julia had assured Pippa that she'd made all the arrangements for her at the hospital where she was going to work after the baby was born, and Pippa had already sent on her medical notes. They wouldn't be expecting her four weeks early, of course, but they would be unlikely to turn her away. Pippa knew that Julia, an obstetrics sister at the hospital, would be at the airport to meet her and would soon have her sorted out.

Pippa got up from her seat and moved towards the back of the plane. The toilet sign on her side of the plane was still comfortingly green. A large lady in a flowery caftan was gathering her things together in preparation for going down the aisle and had actually placed one well-upholstered leg outside her seat. As Pippa lumbered past her, intent only on reaching the privacy of the toilet compartment, she heard the woman's irate voice muttering, 'Do you mind? Some people have no consideration for others!'

Wow, she'd made it! She sank down onto the loo. And then it happened, exactly as she'd dreaded. Her waters broke. The membranes must have ruptured already. It was a good thing she'd got here in time or...

Embarrassing thoughts of how she would have looked if she'd drenched the cool-looking Spanish man sitting next to her flashed into her mind, and for a moment she had to suppress the urge to giggle. She was definitely light-headed now, if she could find that amusing!

She leaned over to the shelves of paper and began a mopping-up operation. The voluminous cotton skirt she'd been wearing since the recent May weather had favoured London with a heatwave was completely soaked. She pulled it off and wrapped it in paper, along with her briefs which were lying on the floor. It was a good thing her enormous white cotton shirt came halfway down her thighs, because at some point she was going to have to emerge from the safety of this place and summon help.

'Are you making your will in there?' Somebody was hammering on the door. 'There's a queue out here and you've been in there far too long!'

Pippa just knew it had to be the large lady who'd been pipped at the post.

'I'm sorry. I need some help. Could you call one of the stewardesses, please?'

Had that really been her own voice? It sounded strange, a bit faint and wobbly. She glanced in the mirror and did a double take. The weird girl with the pale white face who stared back at her, long blonde hair hanging down in damp wispy rats'-tails, didn't resemble her at all. Her blue eyes were red-rimmed and held a hopeless, childlike, lost expression.

She hoped they'd heard her out there. Somewhere in here there was probably a panic button she could press, but she didn't want to resort to anything so dramatic. No, she was going to emerge looking her normal self and—

'Will you open the door, please?'

A different female voice now, with a professional edge to it. That was better! Pippa shot back the bolt.

The stewardess put her arms forward and took hold of Pippa. 'Are you all right?'

'I'm fine,' Pippa said weakly. 'But my waters have broken and—'

'Pass me a blanket!' the woman called to one of her colleagues. 'Let me wrap this round you, Miss Norton.'

So they *had* been keeping tabs on her! They actually knew her name. How efficient these airline staff were.

'Call me Pippa.'

'OK, Pippa, easy does it. If you'd just like to walk with me to the back of the plane…'

The blanket around Pippa restored some of her dignity, but as another contraction occurred she realised that dignity was the last thing she cared about. She doubled up and clung to the side of a seat.

'Just another few steps…' said a soothing voice.

Somehow she made it. Over the loudspeaker system someone was appealing for a doctor.

Pippa sank down onto a chair in the galley section at the back of the plane, taking a deep breath as she looked at the helpful stewardess.

'I'm Carol. According to the information I was given before we took off, you're thirty-six weeks pregnant, aren't you? Now, there's no need to be alarmed, Pippa—'

'I'm not worried,' Pippa said, quickly. 'I'm midwifery trained, so I've delivered quite a few babies myself, but I didn't imagine I'd get to this stage so quickly. The fact that my waters have broken doesn't mean that—'

'I believe you need a doctor. I'm Dr Carlos Fernandez.'

Pippa gave a start as the tall Spanish man who'd been sitting next to her appeared in front of her. His dark brow was furrowed and his expression was one of deep concern as he leaned over her.

Carol pulled a curtain over the aisle behind the doctor, thereby preventing passengers from wandering into the area at the side of the galley.

'This is Pippa, Doctor.'

'We've already met,' the doctor said, in a calm, quiet, charmingly accented voice. 'How many weeks pregnant are you, Pippa?'

Pippa stared up at the doctor, taking comfort from his commandingly confident manner. He looked like the sort of doctor who would know exactly how to cope with this emergency situation.

'Thirty-six weeks.'

A flicker of concern showed in his eyes. 'Thirty-six. I see. Is the baby's father with you? It looks as if your baby is planning an unscheduled arrival.'

Pippa groaned. 'Certainly does! I'm on my own. If only the plane hadn't been delayed I would have— ooh...' Her words tailed off into a loud groan. She realised that this was definitely the point at which she should remember her breathing technique. Through the unreality surrounding her she could hear Dr Fernandez directing the cabin crew. A blanket was spread on the floor, and the doctor was easing her onto it, quietly talking to her in a soothing tone of voice.

'Slowly, slowly, Pippa, that's right. Keep breathing until... Has the pain gone now?'

Pippa opened her eyes, which had been screwed tightly shut as she concentrated on easing her way through the contraction. She nodded at the dark face so near to her own. Seen at close quarters, Dr Fernandez was quite good-looking, really, verging on the handsome in a rugged sort of way.

'I'm going to examine you now, Pippa, so we can

get an idea of how far advanced you are. Have you had any prenatal classes?'

'No, but I'm a trained midwife, so I know what to expect.'

'As a trained midwife flying at thirty-six weeks, you must have been more than a little apprehensive. Was there some reason why you had to fly so late in your pregnancy?'

'My brother died unexpectedly, last month,' she said quietly.

Pippa could feel the tears welling up. She'd kept a tight rein on her emotions ever since Adam's funeral. Somebody had had to provide a shoulder for her mother to cry on. She hadn't intended to let go now, but it was all too much for her. And something in the doctor's sympathetic manner told her that he would be used to tearful patients.

Dr Fernandez, who'd been crouching down to examine her, leaned forward and took hold of her hand.

'I'm sorry your brother died. I suppose that meant your flight had to be delayed until now.' He paused, his eyes searching her face for a reaction. 'It's a pity you couldn't have delayed your baby's birth as well. Your cervix is dilating rapidly now. Very shortly you'll be reaching the stage when you can start to push. Don't push until I tell you, will you?'

'Aagh!' Pippa clung to the doctor's hand as she began breathing again to avoid tensing too much on the strong contraction she was experiencing.

As the contraction receded she realised she was still clinging desperately to the doctor's hand. She released him and he sank back. Looking up at him, she wondered if he was relieved to be released. What on earth must he think of her, causing him so much trouble when probably all he wanted was a nice quiet flight?

'I really am sorry to disrupt your flight like this. I had no idea I was going to go into labour,' she said slowly. 'My obstetrician gave me a certificate to say that I was fit to fly and—'

'Don't worry,' Dr Fernandez said. 'I've delivered babies in more cramped conditions than this before. But this will be my first on an aeroplane.' He hesitated. 'You haven't told me about the baby's father. Will he be at the airport to meet you, or…?'

'My baby's father is in America, Doctor.'

'Ah, I see.'

No, you don't! You don't see at all.

'We're separated.'

Now, why had she said that? She and Ian weren't separated in the accepted sense of the word, which implied a marriage breakdown. Theirs was a breakdown of an affair—a permanent breakdown, if only Ian would come to terms with the situation.

She closed her eyes as she remembered Ian's phone call last night, making a last-ditch attempt to persuade her not to go to Spain. He'd told her he couldn't live without her. He wanted her to change her mind, have the baby in London and then fly out to the States.

'Are you still OK, Pippa?'

Dr Fernandez's concerned voice broke through her thoughts.

She opened her eyes. 'I was just thinking about Ian, my baby's father. He's still hoping I'm going to go out to the States to be near him, and I can't convince him that…'

The doctor leaned forward, his worried expression

showing his concern. 'But surely that would be the best solution to the problem, wouldn't it?'

'Absolutely not! You see, he's married. I didn't know he was married when we started our affair. He claims his marriage is in name only and he's going to get a divorce, but I don't believe him. I've actually seen him out with his wife and children and—'

'He has children of his own?' The doctor looked deeply troubled by this revelation. 'I can see why you couldn't possibly break up his marriage. Love for your children and the family is the most important thing in life. I come from a large, close-knit family myself, and I cannot imagine what it would be like to have a marriage break up. My poor girl, how you must have suffered when you found out that your baby's father wasn't free to marry you!'

The doctor's voice was filled with sympathy. He leaned forward and stroked back the damp strands of hair that had fallen over Pippa's forehead.

'Don't worry, Pippa. I will take care of you,' he said protectively.

Carol had moved nearer to listen in to her life story, but Pippa didn't mind. Everything felt so surreal and, between contractions, it was nice to have a cosy chat with a sympathetic audience. She was tired of bottling things up. Maybe sharing her problems would help to ease some of the pain.

The doctor had taken hold of her hand again. She clung tightly to it as she waited for the next contraction. All she had to do was produce her baby. And take comfort from the strong, confident Dr Fernandez.

She felt a deep attachment to him already as he watched over her with a professional, experienced expression, occasionally checking the state of her birth canal, telling her she hadn't yet reached second stage but it wouldn't be long now. And while all this was going on she just allowed herself to rabbit along as if he were an old friend instead of a perfect stranger.

'You're doing fine, Pippa,' he told her. 'If I had my medical bag with me I could have given you something to ease the pain. I've been over in London at a medical conference and didn't think I'd need it. So all I've got is this woefully inadequate first-aid kit.'

'I'm OK,' she said quickly, squeezing the large, comfortable hand. 'In between the contractions I can relax, so it's not so bad. Now, where was I?'

'You'd just told me that Ian had children.'

'Yes, two boys, ten and twelve. I could never break up a marriage like that, and I certainly don't want to be a mistress for the rest of my life. Ian told me he was divorced when I first met him. A friend enlightened me about his marital status. I was absolutely gutted when I found out, and for a while I couldn't think what I was going to do. I needed to get away, make a new life for myself and the baby…'

She tensed and then tried to relax herself by breathing through the next contraction as it took over with great force. She must be nearly there by now. Surely…

She leaned breathlessly against Dr Fernandez as the contraction stopped. 'That was a horror! Am I anywhere near…?'

The doctor had moved to check on her birth canal. He nodded. 'With the next contraction you can—'

'Thank goodness for that!' Pippa was already bearing down.

She'd never imagined that pushing hard would

come as such a relief. She remembered patients who'd thanked her profusely for saying they could push, but you had to experience it for yourself to appreciate what it was like.

'Stop pushing now and start panting! The baby's head is crowning.'

Pippa did as she was told, realising that her vagina must now be distended to its widest diameter with the crown of the baby's head waiting to pass through it. It was important that the head and face emerge slowly, so as not to endanger the baby. She panted for all she was worth.

'I've got your baby's head now, Pippa. Would you like to see?'

Exhausted as she was, Pippa was able to prop herself up on her elbows and look down at the amazing sight of this wonderful new life. Her darling baby's head was right there, with its wisps of damp blond hair, waiting to make a full appearance onto the stage of life. She could actually hear the baby making a strange, high-pitched cry. How wonderful! In spite of being four weeks early, Matthew's little lungs had developed enough to—

'Wait, wait now, Pippa!'

Dr Fernandez was feeling for the umbilical cord, checking that it wasn't hooked around the baby's neck. Another contraction was coming. Pippa leaned back again as she felt the shift in position of her baby.

'I've got the shoulders and body now...' Dr Fernandez told her as he eased the baby out.

She raised her head. The doctor was cutting the umbilical cord with the airline scissors which Carol had sterilised on the doctor's instructions.

'There you are. It's a boy!'

'I know. It's Matthew. I feel as if I've always known him.'

'He's a wonderful baby! A miracle baby!' Dr Fernandez said, wrapping the precious infant in an airline blanket.

He held Matthew briefly against his body, seemingly unconcerned about the damp state of his shirt.

Pippa looked up at Dr Fernandez, marvelling at the loving, protective concern she saw in his expressive eyes. Even though he must have delivered many babies, he was obviously still deeply moved by the wonder of a new life emerging into the world. Pippa held out her arms towards her tiny son and, even though she'd longed for this moment, she wasn't prepared for the rush of sheer joy that surged over her as Dr Fernandez placed the baby in her arms.

She'd watched as the doctor had swabbed Matthew's eyes and cleansed his nostrils before wrapping him in the towel. The baby felt warm, cuddly. She wanted to hug this precious moment to herself for ever.

'I've never felt so happy in my whole life,' she murmured as she looked down at baby Matthew.

She was only dimly aware that Dr Fernandez had crouched down beside her to deliver the placenta and soon his arm was around her shoulder.

He tightened his fingers. 'Well done, Pippa!'

She looked up and planted a grateful kiss on the side of his dark, stubbly cheek. 'And well done you, Dr Fernandez! I couldn't have done it without you.'

He smiled. 'Oh, I think you could. You're one of those women who's a natural when it comes to having babies. Thank goodness! I don't mind telling you now that you had me worried at first. And we're very lucky that your baby is a good size for a thirty-six-week pregnancy. His breathing is excellent, which was my main concern when he was born. We'll need to check out his lungs again as soon as we land and get into an ambulance. He may need some oxygen. Only a matter of minutes now, so we don't need to worry.' He helped Pippa to a seat and strapped her in, before taking a seat himself, ready for landing.

She held her wonderful baby against her. He snuffled against her, his little rosebud mouth searching hungrily. She smiled and lifted her voluminous shirt so that her precious child could latch on to one of her breasts.

'Isn't Mother Nature wonderful?' Pippa said, as she watched the newborn baby suckling expertly. 'Matthew looks as if he's been here before!'

Dr Fernandez smiled, displaying strong white teeth. 'Maybe he has. Who knows? Why did you choose the name Matthew?'

'It's a family name, from my father and grandfather. Matthew the third.'

Carol, who was now strapped into her own seat, leaned forward. 'Won't it be confusing having three Matthews in the family?'

'Not really.' Pippa swallowed hard. 'Both my father and grandfather have died, so it's up to Matthew to keep the name alive.'

She saw the expression in Dr Fernandez's eyes change and she liked the way he was looking at her now. She saw compassion, admiration, relief…all of those things…and something else she couldn't quite define. A kind of bonding had happened between them at the same time as she'd created the bond with her newborn baby.

But the moment passed as the real world crowded in again.

'I've radioed ahead for the ambulance you ordered, Doctor,' Carol said briskly as she donned her hat and buttoned up her uniform jacket in preparation for emerging from the plane.

'Thank you, Carol.' Dr Fernandez was standing up.

'We're going to take you to my hospital initially, Pippa. You told me your friend will be here to meet you so we can take her along with us.'

'What's your friend's name?' Carol asked. 'I'll arrange for a message to be put out over the tannoy system in the airport.'

'Julia Davidson. She's a nursing sister.'

'Do you mean Sister Davidson from the San Miguel Hospital?' Dr Fernandez asked quickly.

'Yes, do you know her?' Pippa asked.

The doctor smiled. 'I should do. I'm the hospital's medical director.'

Pippa drew in her breath. 'That's where I'm going to work in a few weeks' time. Julia suggested it would be good for me to have a complete change, so I applied for an interview in London and...'

Dr Fernandez ran a hand through his dark hair. 'I've just realised who you are. The name Pippa didn't mean anything to me but I think you must be Staff Nurse Philippa Norton. I believe you're due to start part-time work, aren't you? It's strange that the medical agency in London didn't tell me you would have a baby.'

'Julia assured me that my baby wouldn't be a problem,' Pippa said quickly. 'Julia and I are old friends from our nursing training days and—' She broke off to concentrate on holding her baby against her as the plane came to a halt.

'The ambulance is waiting on the tarmac, Doctor,' Carol said, briskly. 'Sister Davidson has been requested to join you there. We'll take you out through the rear entrance of the plane before the other passengers disembark.'

The passengers were standing up, craning their necks to find out what all the fuss was about as Pippa was stretchered off the plane. A uniformed paramedic had boarded the plane and taken charge of baby Matthew. As she carried him out through the rear exit, a chorus of oohs and aahs went round the plane.

Pippa could hear snippets of excited conversation.

'I told you somebody was having a baby!'

'Was it born on the plane?'

'What did you have, dear?' called the large lady in the flowered caftan who'd berated Pippa for staying too long in the loo. She'd managed to position herself by the rear exit and the cabin staff were having to hold her back.

Pippa waved her hand as the stretcher began its descent of the stairs. 'It's a boy!'

'Good luck, dear!' the woman called back. 'You'll need it. I've got three boys, and they drive me…'

The rest of the sentence was lost. They'd reached the bottom step. And then, all of a sudden, warm arms enveloped her in a friendly hug.

'What a way to arrive in Spain!' Small, plump, dark-haired Julia bent over her friend. 'But then you always liked to make a dramatic entrance.'

'Julia! Thank goodness you're here!'

Relief coupled with an overwhelming feeling of exhaustion swept over Pippa. Trying to be strong was an awful strain on the system!

'How do you feel, Pippa?' Julia asked concernedly.

Pippa gave a wry smile. 'I've felt better. I think I could sleep for a month.'

Julia smiled. 'You'll be lucky! You might want to sleep, but baby will have other ideas. We'll try to give you as much rest as we can while you're in hospital, but after that...'

Pippa's stretcher was being lifted into the ambulance.

'As I was saying,' Julia continued as she sat down beside Pippa, 'we'll keep you in until you feel strong enough to cope. The thing is, you'll be on your own in the apartment. I've moved out.' She lowered her voice as Dr Fernandez moved from the other side of the ambulance. 'Tell you about it later...'

Julia smiled at Dr Fernandez. 'How lucky you were on the plane, Carlos!'

'You didn't tell me your friend was having a baby when we discussed her appointment, Julia.'

'Didn't I? Would it have made any difference?'

The doctor gave her a wry smile. 'Well, I do like to keep tabs on the welfare of my staff. I'll make arrangements for baby Matthew to be cared for in the maternity ward nursery while Pippa is on duty.'

'Yes, I thought that would be the best solution,' Julia said. 'But I was waiting until Pippa actually arrived before I discussed it with you.'

The doctor nodded good-naturedly. 'I'm sure you were, Julia. Well, as Sister in charge of Maternity, it looks as if you've just expanded your responsibilities by one baby.'

He looked down at Pippa as she clutched her tiny

son to her breast. 'I'm glad I'm going to be able to watch Matthew's progress. Having brought him into the world, it would have been such a pity to say good-bye to him after too short a relationship.'

Pippa smiled, her heart full of happiness that stemmed from the birth of her son and meeting up with this wonderful man. She was also glad that her time with Carlos Fernandez was going to be more prolonged than she'd thought.

CHAPTER TWO

'How are you feeling today, Pippa?'

Pippa looked up as she recognised Carlos Fernandez's deep, reassuring voice. She'd been so absorbed with watching little Matthew feed that she hadn't noticed him arrive at the foot of her bed. In his expertly tailored, summer-weight light grey suit, white shirt and striped silk tie, she thought he looked every inch the distinguished medical director.

Not having seen him since being admitted to the ward yesterday, she'd begun to think he'd forgotten all about her, and she was surprised to find just how much that had upset her. She'd found herself longing to talk to him again. She didn't dare to think how awful it would have been if he hadn't been on her plane and she wanted to be able to tell him how grateful she was.

'I'm not so tired now, Dr Fernandez,' she said, feeling unaccustomedly shy in front of the man who had been so wonderful towards her during her labour.

'Please, call me Carlos, Pippa. I feel as if I've known you a long time already.'

Pippa smiled and felt herself able to relax again. 'Thank you so much for taking care of me yesterday. I can't imagine how awful it would have been if...'

He put out his hand and touched her hand. 'Please! I was glad to be able to help you. I would have come in to see you last night but I was called into the operating theatre for an emergency and by the time I was free the night staff said you were asleep.'

'That must have been very late.'

'Well, little Matthew looks fighting fit this morning.' Carlos leaned forward to touch the small blond head as he suckled noisily.

Julia, in her capacity as ward sister, had hurried across from the patient she'd been treating. Carlos turned to look at her.

'Have we checked if baby Matthew is taking colostrum, Julia?'

Julia smiled. 'I think he's getting as much as he needs.'

Pippa felt a certain embarrassment creeping over her as Julia and Carlos stood watching her precious baby suckling as if his life depended upon it.

'Matthew's got to catch up on those last four weeks he missed out on,' she said quietly. 'He's smaller than he would have been if he'd gone to full term so he's making up for lost time.'

Carlos smiled. 'Good point, Pippa. Babies have more intelligence than we give them credit for, and lots of innate natural instinct. He's a sturdy little fellow, considering he didn't make it to full term. I must admit I was relieved his lungs were mature and his breathing was normal when he arrived yesterday.'

He addressed Julia. 'Has Pippa had a full postnatal examination? And baby Matthew?'

Julia nodded. 'Yes, Dr Rodriguez checked both of them soon after they were admitted. I've got the case notes in the office if you'd like to see them.'

'Thank you.' Carlos smiled at Pippa, who was in the middle of changing Matthew from one side to the other. 'Take care of your precious little boy, Pippa, and don't forget to look after yourself. You're just as important as your baby, you know.'

She smiled up at him, revelling in the warmth of feeling flowing from his dark, sympathetic eyes. 'I'll be a model patient.'

'I'm sure you will.'

She watched Carlos following Julia down the ward. He turned and smiled at her before going through the swing doors. She leaned back against the pillows, one hand cradling Matthew's head. Her tiny son had now stopped suckling and was lying absolutely still with an expression of total contentment on his little face. She stroked his head, separating a couple of blond strands that had become tangled together.

He was gorgeous, there was no doubt about it, but then of course she was biased. She hoped he would keep this super-fine blond hair; Ian had dark hair and she wanted to be able to forget him. Oh, she would make sure that Matthew knew who his father was, and that Ian had as much access to his son as he asked for, but their affair was over completely, never to be resurrected.

Pippa smiled to herself as she realised that this was the first time she'd thought about Ian since she'd arrived at the hospital. Good, that meant that baby Matthew wasn't going to be a permanent reminder to her of his father's cavalier attitude to the women in his life.

Carefully, she placed Matthew gently in his cot at the side of her bed, bending to kiss the top of his head. Her thoughts turned to Carlos and Julia, who would be settled in the office. They would probably be having one of those minuscule strong black coffees now as they discussed the patients on the ward and the treatment they were receiving.

She closed her eyes and leaned back against the pillows as she realised how much she was looking forward to getting back to work. She'd taken the last four weeks off, having finished her work as a staff nurse in Accident and Emergency at St Celine's Hospital in London.

It had been a wrench, saying goodbye to all her friends. They'd given her a party in the nurses' home and she'd almost felt like changing her mind and giving up the whole idea of going to Spain. Some of her friends had thought she was completely mad to go out there when she was so heavily pregnant. She'd had to explain why it was such bad timing.

When Julia had written to her with the idea of joining her in the area of Spain where she'd spent so many happy holidays as a child she'd jumped at the idea of making a clean break from Ian, trying to forget that he even existed. At that time she hadn't known she was already pregnant.

At her leaving party, with so many warm-hearted friends sympathetic to the fact that she'd been conned by a master of seduction, she'd wondered if she was making a mistake by uprooting herself from a good job with excellent prospects and loyal colleagues.

But when she'd woken up the morning after the party she'd known she'd made the right decision. Every time she'd walked into hospital she'd been reminded of how Ian had charmed her, with his lies about her being the only girl in the world he could possibly have fallen for. He'd concocted the story that he'd had to divorce his first wife because of her infidelity and hadn't been out with another woman until he'd met her because—

'Are you OK, Pippa?'

Julia's voice broke into her thoughts. She opened her eyes and smiled. 'I'm fine. I was just remembering.'

Julia sat down on the chair at the side of the bed. 'Thinking about Ian, perhaps?'

'How did you know?'

'You were looking a bit sad. Not having second thoughts about ditching him, are you?'

'What do you think? Julia, I couldn't split up his marriage, and I could never live with a man who wasn't to be trusted.'

Julia's voice was full of concern. 'But what about Matthew? Doesn't he have as much right as Ian's other children to be with his father?'

Pippa drew in her breath. She'd known Julia a long time. They'd been drawn to each other on their first day in the preliminary training school when they'd both been raw recruits. Looking at her now, she didn't think Julia had changed much over the years. She'd kept her dark hair in the same short sleek style, and her plump, wrinkle-free face still shone with enthusiasm for life. But she hadn't lost her desire to advise Pippa at every stage in her life, whether the advice was wanted or not.

Pippa pushed her long blonde hair behind her ears. 'Don't worry, I'll make sure Matthew gets to know his father. But I've got to move on with my own life. My affair with Ian is all in the past.'

Julia leaned forward and patted her friend's hand. 'Doesn't it still hurt, the fact that you've split up? I remember how much in love you were at the beginning, when—'

'Don't, Julia! It's seven months since I found out what Ian was really like, and my love just died. When I saw him walking in the park with his beautiful wife, holding her hand while the two boys scurried ahead, kicking a football about...'

She broke off as the memories flooded back. Julia took hold of her hand and squeezed it gently. 'I'm sorry. Please, don't upset yourself. I shouldn't have brought the subject up.'

'And then when I asked around I found out that a couple of my friends in hospital already knew about Ian's marriage but hadn't wanted to disillusion me. They'd hoped it would fizzle out, as his affairs usually did.'

'I didn't know he'd had other affairs, Pippa.'

'I found out that Ian was a serial womaniser. That was one reason why he moved down to London last year from Scotland, and...'

Pippa broke off as she saw Carlos returning down the ward. He came to the side of her bed and stood looking down at her, his expression kindly and sympathetic.

'I've checked out your notes, Pippa, and as far as I can see you should be able to leave hospital in about a week. We're going to keep you in longer than usual, as this wasn't a full-term pregnancy and we need to keep an eye on Matthew. But your health doesn't give us any cause for concern.'

He bent down and stroked Matthew's hair, a tender smile on his lips. 'Matthew is such a special little baby. I want only the best for him. I always feel a distinct bonding with the babies I deliver, and this little treasure is especially wonderful. I know I shouldn't have favourites but…'

Carlos cleared his throat before continuing. 'I understand you're going to be staying with Julia for—?'

'Actually, that's all changed, Carlos,' Julia interrupted as she jumped to her feet.

Pippa watched her friend craning her neck to make her point. She'd seen Julia in this position so many times when they'd worked together in hospital. Julia might be small in stature but she always pulled herself up to her full height, hands on hips, when dealing with tall people, especially senior doctors who had a tendency to underestimate her.

'I've moved out of my apartment so Pippa will have the whole place to herself…and the baby, of course.'

Carlos gave Julia a wry grin. 'Was that because you thought you might not like to have babies all day and all night, Julia?'

'Not at all,' Julia replied quickly. 'I…er…I've moved into another apartment.'

'I see.' The humour had gone but Carlos's enigmatic expression was giving nothing away.

Pippa saw the closed expression on Julia's face. Her friend had only briefly told her about the fabulous boyfriend she'd fallen for, and hadn't given her any details as yet. It was difficult to have a private chat in an open ward. She was looking forward to hearing all the details, but meanwhile the thought of living in a strange apartment with her new baby was slightly daunting. She knew she would be able to cope, but it would have been easier if Julia had been around to show her the ropes.

'Well, if you're going to be on your own, we'd

better make sure you're fighting fit before you leave here,' Carlos said. 'Have you been up and about this morning, Pippa?'

'I went down to the bathroom and took a shower. I felt pretty tired after that so I came back to bed.'

Carlos nodded. 'Very wise. You had a very busy day yesterday.' He gave her a sympathetic smile. 'Take care of yourself and rest when you feel tired. I'll see you later today.'

He leaned over the sleeping baby, placing his hand gently on the fontanelle at the top of Matthew's head. Pippa watched as she saw him feeling for her baby's pulse.

He removed his hand and straightened up to his full height. 'You've got a lovely baby, Pippa.'

Pippa felt a rush of pride, and some other emotion that she couldn't quite quantify. Happiness that Carlos should also have warm feelings towards her darling baby perhaps?

'He seems perfect to me,' she said, quietly, as she looked up at him.

For a moment their eyes met and she felt a shiver running down her spine. Carlos had a kind of charisma that drew her towards him.

'If you'll excuse me, Carlos...' Julia headed off down the ward to berate a junior nurse who'd spilled some water from a flower vase and hadn't mopped it up. 'Just a moment, Nurse!'

Pippa saw an expression of amusement in the doctor's dark eyes. 'Julia hasn't changed at all,' she said quietly.

Carlos smiled. 'She's a very good sister. How long have you known each other?'

'Since we were eighteen.'

'That's about six years, isn't it?'

She laughed. 'You've been checking up on me.'

She was surprised how easy it was to talk to Carlos, as if she'd known him for years. The special bond they'd formed with each other yesterday was still there. You couldn't go through an emergency situation like that without becoming emotionally close.

'It's all in your case notes. Your antenatal record has been in the hospital for the last couple of weeks, so if I'd read that I would have known who you were on the plane. Yes, it's all down there in black and white, I'm afraid, even the fact that your baby's father has abandoned you and—'

'I don't know who wrote that, but it's not true,' Pippa said quickly. 'I've chosen not to continue my relationship with Matthew's father because he's married and has other children. I think I told you about that on the plane.'

'Yes, you did. But sometimes patients in labour become over-emotional and the truth can become distorted. I was just checking what really happened. Hope you don't mind.'

'Not at all.'

Carlos glanced at his watch. 'I'm afraid I've got to go now. I'm due in Theatre in half an hour.'

'Ah, so you actually have to do hands-on work, even though you're the boss here? When you said you were called into Theatre last night I thought it was simply in an administrative capacity.'

Carlos raised one eyebrow. 'You didn't think I was merely an administrator, did you, Pippa?'

'I don't know anything about you,' she said.

A bleeper was sounding in the doctor's pocket.

'Take care of yourself,' he said, before heading off down the ward.

She felt sad as she watched Carlos going out through the swing doors. She enjoyed talking to him, finding out what made him tick, and she would have liked him to stay longer. But he must be a very busy man if he had to run this place and work as a surgeon as well, whereas all she had to do was lie around waiting to feed little Matthew when he was hungry. Perhaps Julia would let her do some light work in a day or two.

Looking around the ward, she reflected that it wasn't very different from the hospital she'd worked in, except that everything was on a smaller scale. She'd been delighted to see how smart and up to date the San Miguel Hospital was when she'd arrived yesterday, and it had amused her to see that it was slap bang in the middle of the fields where that old campsite had been.

Craning her neck to look out across the ward towards the shimmering blue of the sea, she remembered the first time her parents had discovered the campsite. They'd travelled all day in the hot, stuffy car, piled high with sleeping bags from their last stop somewhere in the middle of France. She and Adam had had tins of provisions under their feet as they'd squabbled and argued on the back seat, constantly demanding to know how much further they were going to drive before they could escape the confines of the car.

She was feeling desperately confined herself this morning as she gazed longingly at the sea, remembering how she and Adam had rushed towards it like lemmings the moment their father had unlocked the back doors of the car and—

'You look miles away!' Julia said, leaning across the bed.

Pippa smiled. 'Actually, I was right here, on this very spot. It used to be a campsite, you know. I told you we'd stayed at San Miguel when I was a child, didn't I?'

Julia's eyes twinkled. 'Oh, yes, I'm perfectly aware that you didn't come down here to see me. It was simply to renew happy memories of your childhood.'

Pippa laughed. 'Rubbish! But I must admit that as soon as I realised where you were working I knew I was going to like it down here.'

Julia straightened the cover on Pippa's bed, tucking in the corner of the sheet with professional precision.

'Has it changed much, Pippa?'

'From the brief glimpse I got when we arrived, it looks as though there's been a lot of building, but they haven't changed the character of the place. There are no high-rise apartments or hotels spoiling the view of the sea.'

Julia nodded. 'All the holiday chalets have been built in the pine forest, higher up the hill. And the extended campsite is tucked away around the corner of the cliff in the next bay.'

'I hope the farmer who ran the old campsite got a good price for the land where they built the hospital. He was a good man, always so helpful when we needed anything,' Pippa said, feeling a tug of nostalgia in the pit of her stomach. 'We always had great holidays here.'

Julia touched her hand. 'It must have been awful for you, losing your only brother,' she said in a quiet, sympathetic voice. 'When I heard what had happened I thought you were very brave to stick to your original plan of coming out here.'

Pippa leaned back against the pillows as the awful shock of her brother's accident hit her once again. 'I was more concerned about what it would do to Mum when it actually happened. I knew I could cope, but Mum understandably went to pieces. I needed to be strong for her.'

Julia nodded understandingly. 'Your father's death and then the loss of her only son in such a short space of time must have been…well…'

She broke off, spreading her hands wide as if to express that it was beyond her comprehension.

'The trouble is,' Pippa said slowly, 'Mum still feels guilty about Dad's death. She's convinced he drove his car off the road on purpose.'

'But didn't the coroner say it was because of the dense fog that—?'

'You try telling my mother! She's convinced that it was because she'd left Dad to go and live with Mike.' Pippa took a deep breath as she felt tears pricking behind her eyes. 'So it hit Mum hard when Adam was killed in the Alps.'

'A climbing accident, wasn't it?' Julia asked.

Pippa nodded, momentarily unable to speak as she tried once more to come to terms with what had happened to her family in the last couple of years—first her mother leaving her father, then her father's death and most recently the death of her brother. Around her, the sound of crying babies and mothers soothing or feeding them reminded her that life went on, even after the darkest days she'd had to go through.

'I was so sorry when you phoned me. I'm glad you

didn't change your plans, because I'm sure you'll be happier here than you would be in London. You're going to love working here. It's a really friendly hospital.'

Pippa took a deep breath. 'Talking of which—perhaps I could help out on the ward a little, maybe tomorrow?'

Julia smiled. 'We'll see how you are. You need to get some rest, my girl. I feel a bit guilty about leaving you on your own in the flat, but—' she lowered her voice '—I was persuaded it was all for the best.'

'You're being very mysterious about this, Julia,' Pippa said. 'When are you going to let me into the secret?'

A young English nurse had hurried over to Pippa's bedside with a tray on which she'd prepared a sedative for Julia to double-check. Julia checked over the medication and nodded her approval. 'That's fine, Naomi.'

She turned back to Pippa, lowering her voice again. 'As you can see, I can't discuss my private life on the ward, Pippa. When you're up and about tomorrow, come and have coffee in the office. I can also explain about how the hospital works, the staffing arrangements and so on.'

'I've noticed that you've got more English nurses than Spanish on this ward.'

'Yes, we've got a lot of English staff in the rest of the hospital as well, both doctors and nurses. When there was a rapid increase in the number of English visitors and people looking to buy houses in this area, the hospital did a recruitment drive based in London. The reason the hospital was built in the first place was because of the influx of tourists and permanent overseas residents.'

'I was hoping to learn something about the Spanish culture.'

'Oh, you'll get that when you go to live in the apartment. It's in the middle of the village, so you'll be well and truly in with the local people. How's your Spanish?'

Pippa smiled. 'I've been working on it.' She pointed to the phrase book on her bedside locker. *'Tengo que trabajar mucho para hablar español.'*

'Well done! Good accent you've got. Roughly translated you said, "I must work hard to speak Spanish," didn't you? Where did you learn that?'

'At school, actually. Adam and I used to try out a few phrases when we were on holiday here, but I've got a long way to go before I'm fluent.'

'Keep practising!' Julia smiled as she moved away.

'I will,' Pippa said and she reached down into the cot to lift out her son.

Matthew had been snuffling his little chin around the light cotton cover for a few minutes but Pippa hadn't wanted to take him out too soon. His thin wailing cry now alerted her to the fact that he was hungry again, or maybe just needed reassurance that his mummy was still there. She held him against her, revelling in the warm feeling of his little body. Her precious son. They had a lifetime to get to know each other and the adventure had only just begun.

It was a relief to be up and about, actually moving around the ward the next day. Julia had asked Pippa simply to chat to some of the more inexperienced English mothers who were having problems with feeding their babies. One young girl in particular seemed greatly relieved when Pippa asked if she would like some help.

'I'm midwifery trained,' Pippa explained as she sat down on the chair at the side of the bed. 'So I've had a lot of experience with feeding problems. You've got a lovely baby there.'

The young mother raised an eyebrow. 'He's lovely at the moment, but you must have heard him screaming in the night.'

'We all heard him screaming,' a deep masculine voice said. 'I came along from my office to see if the night staff could calm him down.'

Pippa looked up as she heard Carlos's voice. 'I wouldn't have thought you had to work nights, Carlos.'

He looked down at her, a solemn expression on his dark, handsome face. 'It was only midnight. Sometimes I'm here much longer if there's emergency surgery to perform.'

She smiled. 'I'm impressed.'

Carlos shrugged. 'All part of the job.'

'I suspect you enjoy it.'

'I do.' He turned his attention to the young patient. 'Sister tells me that Staff Nurse Pippa is going to give you some tips on breastfeeding, Melissa. Pippa is an expert, so I think you'll find her very helpful.'

'I wish she'd feed him for me! I find the whole thing so boring,' Melissa said. 'Boring, messy—'

She broke off as she saw the look of concern on the doctor's face. 'I'm following the hospital's advice by breastfeeding him, but I'd much rather put him on the bottle.'

'You can do that if you prefer,' Pippa said. 'But

we always like to give baby a good start in hospital. It's up to you. He's your baby, but it really is worth persevering with breastfeeding. Mother's milk is so good for baby.'

Glancing up at Carlos, she saw he was smiling down at her, an expression of approval on his handsome face.

'When you actually start work here I'm sure you will prove to be a great asset,' he said quietly. He glanced at his watch. 'Got to go. Goodbye for now.'

Pippa drew in her breath as she watched him walking away. His fascinatingly accented English intrigued her. She was glad to find that Carlos seemed to approve of her, and surprised to find that it really mattered to her what this doctor, in his commanding, enigmatic, quintessentially Spanish way, thought about her.

Working in a hospital in London she'd always done her job to the best of her ability, regardless of what people thought about her. Even when she'd been at the full height of her affair with Ian, and he'd been a consultant on the ward where she was working, she hadn't stopped to worry about whether he would approve of her work or not. But there was something about Dr Carlos Fernandez that tore at her heartstrings. Underneath that calm, confident exterior there was a vulnerability that she seemed to tap into every time she was near him.

She leaned over the cot and picked up Melissa's baby, who was now screaming loudly.

'There there, Anthony,' she whispered as she handed the baby to his mother. 'Mummy's going to feed you now. Hold him against you like this,

Melissa…yes, just guide his mouth over your nipple… Let me show you…'

It was difficult at first, but Pippa found that Melissa was getting the hang of things after a couple of minutes, though baby Anthony screamed in protest at the maddening inexperience of his mother.

As he finally sucked hungrily Melissa gave a sigh of relief. 'I never thought it would be as hard as this. The birth yesterday was ten times worse than I imagined. But at least it's all over with now. If I get the hang of this feeding lark it won't be half as much trouble as making up feeding bottles, will it? My mum says she's not going to give me any help. She's got her own kids to worry about.'

'Do you live out here?' Pippa asked carefully.

'I do now. I was in the middle of my last year at school in England when I got pregnant. My mum's living out here with her second husband so my dad sent me here to have the baby. He said he couldn't cope with an expectant mum at home. Mum wasn't too pleased to see me either. She's got her hands full with Jason and Rebecca, her two-year-old twins, not to mention the fact that she's in the club again.'

Anthony started bawling as Melissa moved too quickly. Pippa leaned forward and guided the little mouth until he latched on again.

'I've known so many mothers who didn't want to breastfeed and then couldn't understand why they'd felt like that after a few days,' Pippa said gently. 'I think you're going to be one of those.'

Melissa brightened. 'Do you really think so?'

'If you're determined to make it work for you, it will…Yes, Sister?'

Pippa smiled as she looked up at Julia.

'I wonder if you could tear yourself away and come down to the office for a few minutes?'

Pippa looked at Melissa. 'I'll be back soon, to see how you're getting on.'

'And how is Melissa getting on?' Julia asked, as they walked down the ward together.

'I've been trying to persuade her it will be good for her and the baby if she can persevere with the breastfeeding. I think we may have a convert.'

'Good. Thanks for helping out. It's so important to sort out feeding problems from the beginning.'

Julia pushed open the door to her office. Pippa was surprised to see Carlos sitting in one of the armchairs, his long legs sprawled out in front of him almost tripping her up as she went in.

'So this is your hideaway,' Pippa said, looking around the small room. A desk in one corner held a computer and a pile of case notes. Two armchairs were pushed against the walls, along with a couple of hard-backed chairs.

'Looks like a doctor's waiting room, but I have made the effort to personalise it,' Julia said, waving her hand towards the geranium plant at the corner of one of the occasional tables that cluttered up the centre of the office.

'Very cosy,' Pippa said. 'It reminds me of all the cluttered nursing offices we've ever inhabited together.'

Julia laughed. 'Would you like coffee or tea?'

'I'd better have tea,' Pippa said. 'It's got less caffeine than coffee and I don't want Matthew to become hyperactive.'

Julia's expression was one of amazement. 'I never

thought I'd see the day when you gave up your caffeine fix. It used to be intravenous coffee from early morning till late at night.'

Pippa laughed. 'It's early days. When I'm coping on my own with baby Matthew in the big wide world I may succumb once more.'

She smoothed down the creases in the skirt of her cotton dress. Having been unable to unpack her case completely, she'd taken out the first garment that came to hand. Out there on the ward she'd felt she was reasonably dressed, but now, in the confines of the office, with the impeccably suited hospital director and Julia in her smart navy blue sister's uniform, she felt decidedly under-dressed.

'So what's this news you're going to tell me, Julia?' Carlos said, evenly. 'I've only got a couple of minutes to spare so you'd better make it quick.'

'OK, here goes.' Julia hesitated. 'I thought I'd tell Pippa at the same time. Well, actually I needed some moral support. You see, I've moved in with Pablo Rodriguez and I wondered how the hospital authorities would view this. We were going to keep it secret, but apparently the hospital grapevine is buzzing so I thought I'd get in first with the news.'

Carlos remained silent for a few moments, as if considering his words carefully before he committed himself.

'There's no ruling on private living arrangements. The problem here is that Dr Rodriguez has a wife in Barcelona.' He paused and drew in his breath. 'So long as you're discreet about the relationship there is no reason why both of you shouldn't continue to work here.'

Carlos stood up and moved towards the door. 'Thank you for telling me. I have to go now.'

As the door closed, Pippa looked at Julia. 'This wouldn't be a problem in London, would it?'

Julia nodded. 'I thought long and hard before I agreed to moving into Pablo's apartment. He's assured me his marriage is over.'

Pippa felt a shiver of apprehension running down her spine. That was what Ian had always told her. She hoped that Julia wasn't going to suffer as she had.

'Pablo and I are so much in love,' Julia said, her eyes shining with excitement as she mentioned her boyfriend's name. 'I know it's going to be OK. Just living together is wonderful!'

'I hope you'll be very happy,' Pippa said, fervently wishing that it would be so.

CHAPTER THREE

PIPPA manoeuvred Matthew's pram over the rough cobblestoned road. There was no pavement in this part of the village and it wasn't easy to push this flimsy contraption. It had been the only one available at the second hand shop in the village when she'd come out of hospital, and, as she reminded herself once more, beggars couldn't be choosers.

Looking down at the provisions she'd bought from another of the colourful village shops, or *tiendas*, as she'd learned to call them, some on the tray underneath, others packed around Matthew's feet, not to mention the heavy bag swinging from the pram handle, she knew she was definitely overloaded.

Thank goodness Matthew had at last gone to sleep! Having kept her awake half the night, he now seemed in angelic mood again.

She paused for a moment, to give herself a rest from pushing the heavy pram. Her back was aching and the morning sun beating down on her head was causing moist patches of perspiration on her face. She was glad she hadn't attempted to apply any make-up. Not that it would have been easy, with Matthew bawling his head off. A quick swipe with the sunscreen over her face and some moisturing protection for her lips had been all she'd achieved before fixing Matthew into his pram.

She took her hands off her second hand contraption to reach into her shoulder bag for a tissue. The weight

45

of the bag on the handle caused the pram to topple forward, spilling packages over her feet.

'Ouch!' Leaning forward, she held on to Matthew, who opened his eyes and started to moan with annoyance at being disturbed.

'I'm sorry, Matthew, but...'

'Do you need some help?'

'You could say that!' Pippa glanced up in surprise and embarrassment at the sound of Carlos Fernandez's voice. He was the last person she'd expected to meet in the village!

What would he think of her now! Inept, to say the least, and foolish to try and carry so much stuff all in one go. She began to unbuckle the strap that crossed over Matthew, lifting him out and holding him against her to try and soothe the loud sobbing.

'These prams aren't really meant to carry much beside a baby,' Carlos said gently.

'I know that!' she said wearily. 'But when you've had very little sleep, and then you realise you haven't got any food in the house...'

She broke off as she watched the doctor's expression change to one of sympathetic concern.

'OK, Pippa,' he said, soothingly. 'Let me hold Matthew for a while until you've sorted out this contraption.'

She felt herself relaxing as she listened to his quiet voice. It was three weeks since she'd been discharged from hospital and she'd really missed Carlos's calming influence on her.

As she rearranged the provisions in the pram she was aware of Carlos's voice as he persuaded Matthew to become a calm, happy baby again. The crying had stopped and Matthew was now gurgling happily.

Holding firmly to the handle of the pram, she glanced up at the doctor and saw the animation in his expression as he talked to her baby.

'Yes, you're a beautiful baby,' he was saying softly. 'And haven't you grown since you decided to appear in the aeroplane?'

Pippa watched in fascination, seeing Carlos's obvious delight in looking after Matthew.

He turned to smile at her. 'Come on, let's get you home. The apartment isn't too far, is it? I remember where it is from when Julia lived there. If you'd like to push the pram, I'll carry Matthew. He seems happier to be held than put down in the pram.'

'Thanks.' Pippa felt calmer now that someone else was taking charge. 'I'm just so tired at the moment; it was the last straw when this thing collapsed on me.'

'Matthew not sleeping too well?'

'He definitely prefers to play at night and sleep during the day at the moment.'

'He's only four weeks old so the pattern could change when…'

'*Buenos días*, Dr Fernandez!'

A diminutive old lady, leaning heavily on her stick, had moved from the doorway of her white-painted village house. Her wrinkled face creased into a happy smile as she reached forward to touch the baby that the doctor was holding.

Pippa smiled at the old lady as she chatted amicably with the doctor, and from her limited Spanish gathered that she was admiring the beautiful baby. Dr Fernandez was now fielding questions about when he was going to get married and have babies of his own. Pippa tried hard to follow the conversation, but the only part she really understood was that there was someone called Maria who had an important part in his life.

She'd been surprised—and strangely relieved—when she'd first discovered he wasn't married. There was something about him that appealed to her enormously. It was inevitable, though, that he would have a girlfriend, or possibly a fiancée. Julia had told her Dr Fernandez was thirty-two, so he was probably reaching the age when marriage wasn't far away.

'Adios, señora.' Carlos began to move away. Pippa, adding her own, 'Adios señora,' followed, trundling the pram.

She stopped in front of the old white-painted two-storey house where she was now living in the downstairs apartment. Putting her key in the door, she turned it. Carlos pushed it open and stood back to let her go inside.

Parking the pram in the narrow hall, she held out her arms towards Matthew, who was now fast asleep again. Carlos gently handed her the baby and stood quietly in the doorway. Pippa began to thank him for helping her, but all the time she was wondering whether she dared ask him in. She was reluctant to see him go so soon. She'd felt so grim when she'd left the house this morning but now she was feeling almost human again. Even her back had stopped aching.

'Would you like a cold drink?'

She saw him hesitate. She was sure he was going to turn down her offer. 'I've got a juicer, and I've just bought some fresh oranges. I'll put Matthew down in his cot and then...'

'Fruit juice would be a good idea. I'll make it while you settle your baby.'

She tiptoed through into the bedroom, laying Matthew down as gently as she could so as not to waken him.

'Please don't wake, Matthew,' she whispered, stroking the blond hair as she put a thin cotton cover over him. 'I love you dearly, but I need a few minutes' adult company.'

She glanced at herself in the mirror. She'd lost her pregnancy weight already. In fact if the truth be known she was a bit on the thin side again. Only her breasts remained larger than they normally were. She tied the belt of the cream cotton frock she'd bought in the village market last week. It was too big for her, but infinitely suitable for shopping in the village, which was good. She wanted to become accepted in the community, not to be regarded as a tourist.

There was no point doing anything to her shiny face, although she did grab a lipstick and apply a quick swipe. The hasty chignon she'd achieved in the early hours of the morning was losing all its hairgrips. Impatiently, she pulled the remaining grips out of it and gave a few strong strokes with the brush to her shoulder-length blonde hair.

Carlos held out a glass of orange juice towards her as she hurried into the small kitchen at the back of the apartment.

'Sorry you had to make your own drink, Carlos. Incidentally, why are you away from the hospital to-day?' she added over her shoulder as she led the way through the living room to the terrace.

'I'm having a weekend off,' he said, settling him-self into one of the wicker chairs.

'I'd forgotten it was Saturday,' she said, choosing a chair next to him. 'All the days seem the same at the moment. And because I'm often awake half the night I tend to lose track of time.'

Carlos leaned forward. 'I'm worried about you, Pippa. You shouldn't be alone like this for days on end.'

'Oh, I do take Matthew out as much as I can. We walk to the shops, and we go down to the sea and sit on the beach sometimes. He's too young to appreciate how beautiful it all is, but...'

Her voice trailed away as her eyes met his. 'I'm not fooling you, am I, Carlos? Yes, I admit I am finding it hard to live here with my new baby. Yes, I sometimes wish I was back in England, and...'

She tried to hold back the tears, but they came anyway. The next thing she knew, large, comforting arms were holding her.

'It's OK, Pippa. You've been through a difficult time and you're going to need help until you're really strong again. Look, I've got plenty of time today, so why don't you go and have a rest? When Matthew wakes up I'll give him a bottle. I notice you're fully equipped in the kitchen for supplementary feeding, so off you go and get your head down.'

She stared at Carlos. 'That would be wonderful. But I warn you, I might sleep the clock round. You'd better wake me when you want to go.'

He smiled. 'That's fine. Don't worry. Having brought young Matthew into the world, I feel very much responsible for his welfare—and I don't want him to be looked after by an exhausted mother.'

Through the mists of consciousness Pippa became vaguely aware that Matthew was snuffling around in his cot beside her bed, the first stage before he would begin his outright screaming for her attention. She tried to open her eyes, but the eyelids seemed unnaturally heavy. She would give herself another few seconds of blissful sleep before she...

A miracle was happening! Somebody was lifting Matthew from his cot, whispering soothing words to him as he was spirited away. Opening one eye, she saw Carlos disappearing through the bedroom door, complete with baby. And then she remembered the wonderful arrangement he'd suggested, that she was to sleep on until she awakened and he would take care of...

She was already falling back into the depths of a luxurious sleep...

It was already dark when she became conscious again. Someone was standing beside her bed. She started as she saw the outline of a man.

'Carlos! What time is it? How long have I...?'

'Don't worry. I just came in to check you were all right.'

She sat up quickly, too quickly. Her head was spinning. She sank back against the pillows. 'Do you have to go?'

Carlos sat down on the side of her bed and reached for her hand. The touch of his fingers unnerved her, even though she soon realised that he was merely taking her pulse.

'No, I don't have to go if you'd like me to stay a little longer. Are you hungry?'

'I suppose I am,' she said slowly. 'I never really think about it nowadays. I know I should pay more attention to my diet, but...'

He squeezed her hand in a friendly gesture. 'Yes,

you should, with a baby to feed and your own health to build up. You're looking a bit thin, and a rapid weight-loss after the birth of a baby isn't...'

'I know, I know. The theory of motherhood is all very well, but when you have to put it into practice...'

'You've been unlucky in your choice of father, that's all, but this evening I'll play father to Matthew and you can relax. I'm planning to have dinner at my favourite restaurant and I would be honoured if you and Matthew would be my guests.'

Pippa's mouth began to water at the thought of it. And she was still intrigued with the way Carlos spoke in his gallant, charming Spanish accent. 'We'd love to, but what if Matthew starts howling?'

'No problem! The staff will take him into the kitchen and spoil him rotten. We're in Spain, not England, remember?'

Pippa laughed. Carlos's boyish enthusiasm was infectious. How little she knew about him. Perhaps tonight she would get to know what the real Carlos was like.

'Matthew is asleep in his pram in the living room,' he continued in his rapid, perfectly correct English. 'So don't disturb him. I'll go home—I don't live far from here—so that I can shower and change. Matthew deposited some of his feed on my shirt, as you can see, or rather smell! I'll be back about nine.'

'Nine!' That was the time she was usually falling asleep these days! What with the heat and the continual round of babycare, she felt dead on her feet when the evening came. But today she'd had that lovely long sleep and, coupled with the buzz she was getting from being with the charismatic Carlos, she would probably be OK.

'We always eat late in Spain,' Carlos told her. 'After sunset, when the cool of the evening descends—that's the time to go out and enjoy yourself. So you've got plenty of time to get ready.'

She watched him going out through the door, his jaunty step helping to put her in the mood for this unexpected evening. What a charming man he was! She climbed off the bed and went over to the vast wooden wardrobe. She'd inherited a lot of wardrobe space with this apartment. Far more than she needed.

She'd deliberately chosen to sleep in the second bedroom, because Julia still had some stuff in the main one. Her friend was constantly promising to remove it, but it hadn't happened yet. She'd gathered from her infrequent flying visits that between working at the hospital and pursuing her affair with Pablo there was very little time left to attend to mundane problems. Pippa had insisted on taking over the rent of the apartment, which was actually very reasonable, and Julia's name had been replaced on the contract.

Looking in the wardrobe now, she realised she would have to buy some more clothes to see her through the hot summer months. Finally she chose the cream silk dress she'd worn for her mother's wedding last year. It was smart, without being over the top. She'd felt it was appropriate at the wedding, and she'd been able to wear it a few times after that.

Thinking of her mother now, she hoped she wasn't still depressed about Adam's death. On the phone the other evening she'd seemed a bit tearful, but she'd said that Mike was being very helpful. Pippa was relieved that the marriage seemed to be working out. Her mother had asked when she would be able to see her grandson, and Pippa had thrown out an open invitation for her mother and her husband to visit, explaining that she wouldn't be coming back to England for a while.

It was a matter of pride to her that she should stick it out, even though she'd been tempted to go back home a few times. Especially in the dark hours of the night, when she was trying to soothe Matthew back to sleep and she felt so terribly alone.

But not so alone that she would want to take up the offer Ian made to her on the phone a couple of nights ago. She wished she hadn't had to give him her phone number, but he'd insisted he wanted to keep in touch with his son. Fair enough, but that was as far as it was going to go. Ian could repeat as often as he liked how he could set her up in an apartment, all expenses taken care of, including paying for her flight over to the States. Even when she was feeling at her lowest she wasn't tempted in the slightest.

She stepped into the shower, and as she rubbed shampoo into her hair, she smiled to herself as the song about washing that man right out of her hair came into her mind. Ian was history as far as she was concerned, and she was moving on.

She reached through the shower curtain to grab a towel. Everything would seem better when she was allowed to start work at the hospital. There would be no problem with baby Matthew. When she was working he would be cared for.

As she came stepping out of the shower she heard Matthew crying. For once she welcomed the sound, because it meant she could feed him before going out and that would make her breasts more comfortable. She flung on her cotton housecoat and padded barefoot into the living room.

Matthew's little rosebud mouth closed around her nipple and he gave a sigh of content, his big blue eyes watching her face as she chatted quietly to him.

'I'm sorry you had to have that bottle, darling, but Mummy was oh, so tired, and the nice kind Dr Carlos said he would…'

Matthew had closed his eyes now, as if bored by her chattering. Pippa hoped she wasn't sending him off to sleep before he'd taken enough milk. She smiled down at him. At four weeks he was still co-cooned in his own little uncomplicated world. Soon he would begin to develop his personality and they would begin to communicate more easily with each other. And she was looking forward to the day when he would begin to talk.

Yes, being a mum was so exciting. Settling him down in his pram after changing and feeding him, she glanced at the clock. Only ten minutes to get ready.

The doorbell rang. Please don't let that be Carlos! But who else could it be?

Carlos stood on the threshold, smiling down at her. Outside in the road was a superb silver car and, surprise surprise, a young man in a smart dark suit was sitting in the driver's seat.

She clutched at the front opening of her flimsy robe with one hand whilst she ran the other hand over her damp hair.

'I'm afraid I'm not ready. Matthew needed feeding. You'd better come in. I'll be about five minutes.'

Carlos smiled. 'No hurry. Take your time, Pippa.'

She noticed that he was looking decidedly smart this evening. His lightweight dark grey suit was immaculate in cut and style. She began to wonder about this restaurant they were going to. If it was Carlos's favourite then it was probably a very elegant place. She glanced at the beautiful car and the man at the wheel.

'What about your friend? Wouldn't he...?'

'That's Pedro, my driver. He prefers to stay in the car and listen to the radio. Don't worry about him.'

A driver! 'How far is it to this restaurant?' she asked as she ran up the stairs.

'Too far to walk for a lady with a baby, I think. Pedro always drives me if I'm going to drink wine. I'll settle Matthew in the car while you're getting ready,' Carlos said, lifting the baby from his pram.

'Oh, no, don't disturb him yet. He...'

'Too late. I already have. Matthew and I haven't had a chat for hours, so it will give us a chance to catch up with each other. Who's a good little boy, then? Who's going to go out with Mummy and Carlos for a lovely evening and...?'

Matthew was snuggling himself against Carlos as he listened to the soothing sound of his voice.

Pippa smiled. 'I'll see you both in the car.'

As she ran up the stairs she began to feel a certain apprehension about the evening. It was all very well for Carlos to say that the restaurant staff would love Matthew, but what if they didn't? Carlos might be able to relax, but she was the baby's mother, and responsible for him twenty-four hours a day. And would Matthew become upset at being taken into a strange car without her?

She needn't have worried. All was calm and peaceful when she rushed out to the car. The driver was waiting for her, holding open the door to the back seat. Carlos was sitting at the far side and Matthew, now asleep again, had been strapped into a car seat between them.

'*Caramba!*' Carlos exclaimed as she climbed in, trying to be as elegant as was possible considering the high-heeled sandals she wasn't used to and the tight silk skirt of her dress with the long slit at the back. 'What a transformation! This can't be the weary young mother I met up with in the village this morning. You look wonderful, Pippa!'

'Thank you.' Already she was feeling better. 'I didn't know you had a car seat for Matthew.'

'With four married sisters my house resembles a nursery at times. We have every conceivable piece of baby equipment imaginable. I'm living in the family house, so my sisters still regard it as home when they come to stay. And I have a much better pram than the difficult one you have at present, which I will lend you—if you like,' he added carefully.

'Thank you. I'd like that very much…if your sisters won't need it for a few months.'

'Don't worry. Their babies are growing up now.' He hesitated. 'So, you really are planning to stick it out here?'

Pippa nodded. 'It will be better when I start working. That was the reason for coming out here.' She hesitated. 'I don't suppose I'd be allowed to start sooner than my contract states?'

They were driving up the steep hill that led out of the village. The smell of the pine trees drifted in through the open windows. Suddenly it seemed very important that she should get back into action again. Wonderful as motherhood was; it shouldn't be all-consuming. She still needed to be part of the real world of work and use the nursing skills she'd acquired.

Carlos was looking thoughtful. 'It's important that you rest, Pippa. You'd be no good to the patients if you were tired.' He paused. 'On the other hand, you do need more of a life than you've got at present. Perhaps you could work a couple of hours each morning on the maternity ward. Matthew will be in the ward nursery while you're working so you won't have to worry about him. What do you think?'

Pippa smiled. 'I think that would be wonderful! But would you be able to organise that?'

Carlos stroked Matthew's blond hair gently. 'I can do anything for baby Matthew. And making his mother happy is therefore one of my priorities.'

She leaned back against the leather seat and closed her eyes. Matthew's car seat between them obscured Carlos's vision of her. It was wonderful to feel pampered like this, but at the same time she didn't want to feel that Carlos was taking care of her only for the sake of Matthew's welfare. She realised, with a rush of surprise, that, wonderful as Carlos's intentions were, she wanted more. She wanted Carlos to like her for herself. She wanted to form a proper relationship with him, not just to be an appendage to her baby son.

She looked out of her side window and caught a final glimpse of the crescent-shaped beach leading to the harbour. From this angle she could still see the lights from the local fishing boats moored alongside the visiting yachts. They were reaching the top of the hill, where the road flattened out across the rolling plain leading to the foothills of the Pyrenees. By the light of the moon she could vaguely distinguish the occasional roadside tree, but the rest of the country-side was in darkness.

'We're almost there,' Carlos said, pointing to where lights beckoned in the distance.

Pedro drove the car through stone-pillared gates. It looked as if they were approaching a country house. The car stopped, and Pedro got out and came around to open the back door for Pippa. As she stepped out she was thinking that she could very easily get used to this! There was nothing like a bit of luxurious living to improve the way you looked at the world!

She gazed up at the impressive façade of the ancient stone building. It was more like a castle than a restaurant! She turned back to lift Matthew out, but Carlos was already unfastening the whole seat.

'I'll carry Matthew in his car seat, Pippa. He will be more comfortable lying in it while we have dinner.'

A tall, slim lady of a certain age, wearing an elegant black dress, came out of the front door and made her way across the drive to the car.

'*Bienvenido!* Welcome!' She stretched out her hands towards the baby, exclaiming in delight.

Pippa didn't understand everything that was said, but gathered that the lady was on the staff of the restaurant and that Carlos had told her on the phone he was bringing a baby with him. Apparently she wanted to take charge of the baby so that they could enjoy their dinner.

Pippa's apprehension about handing Matthew over to a complete stranger and watching him disappearing into the interior of the house was dispersed when Carlos assured her that he'd known the lady of the house for years. Apparently she was used to him accompanying his sisters, with their numerous children, and her feelings would be hurt if she wasn't allowed to take care of this baby.

Pippa could feel herself relaxing. It was all too good to be true. Carlos took hold of her hand and placed it through his arm. 'Well, are you ready to go in now, *señorita*?'

As she smiled up at him she thought how handsome he looked in the moonlight. It was a clichéd situation. The soft lights from the front of the house and the moon up above.

'I feel as if I've died and gone to heaven,' she murmured, almost under her breath. 'It looks such a smart place. I didn't have time to get ready properly. Do you think I look...?'

Carlos bent down and touched her cheek briefly with his lips. 'You look beautiful, Pippa. Stop worrying.'

The touch of his lips excited her. He was probably only being gallant. It didn't mean a thing to him. This was the way he would escort his sisters. But for this evening she was going to imagine that he was escorting her, not out of a sense of duty but because he wanted to be with her. Somehow her natural confidence and self-esteem had been eroded since she'd had baby Matthew. Because Matthew was the most important part of her life now she'd forgotten how to be a woman in her own right.

A phrase sprang to mind. She should get out more! It was so very true. And in that moment she began to realise that she was on the road to recovery. Yes, she was Matthew's mum, but she had to make a real life for herself and regain her self-confidence.

They sat at the bar, and Pippa heard the noise of a cork popping out of a champagne bottle.

'Do you think I should drink this, Carlos?' She eyed the foaming champagne glass that had been placed in front of her.

Carlos smiled. 'I wouldn't give it to you if I thought it would hurt Matthew, would I? One glass of champagne is allowed for nursing mothers. Only ten per cent of the alcohol will reach the baby. After you've drunk this you can go on to mineral water.'

'Thank you, Doctor,' she said with mock solemnity as she raised the glass to her lips.

'Salud! Good health!' Carlos clinked his glass against Pippa's.

CHAPTER FOUR

THEIR corner table by the window looked out over the floodlit garden, from where the heady scent of roses wafted in through open casement windows. Pippa looked around the large, high-ceilinged, wood-panelled room with its impressive crystal chandeliers.

The clientele was mostly distinguished-looking Spanish men in smart suits with elegant, dark-haired, immaculately coiffured ladies. There were a couple of family tables, with children seated around their parents and grandparents, enjoying the convivial ambience of the restaurant and exhibiting absolutely no problem with the generation gaps.

Pippa felt a pang of envy towards such a delightfully easy family lifestyle. How wonderful it would be to have her own family! To sit at that round table over there as the matriarch of a clan like that! But to achieve such a dream you had to work at it. In the first instance you had to choose the right man to father your children, and in that respect she'd failed at the first hurdle.

This wasn't the sort of place she and her family had frequented in their early camping days. Money had always been tight, she remembered, and they had mostly cooked their own food on the campsite: sausages, eggs—always eggs, because they were cheap—and tomatoes. And the atmosphere around the camping table had been a million miles from the sort of convivial ambience surrounding the family on the table close by.

The incompatibility of her parents had always been blatantly obvious to Pippa. From a very early age she'd known that it was only a question of time before they split up. So a warm family life was something she'd longed for but never experienced at first hand.

She glanced at Carlos as he was instructing the waiter about the wine he'd chosen. In those faraway days she would never have dreamt that she would one day be sitting in a restaurant like this with such a distinguished-looking man as her escort. Distinguished, charismatic, and utterly fanciable!

Steady on! She could feel herself in danger of falling in love with the man if she wasn't careful. And he was only being kind to her, a stranger in his country. He'd been so terribly correct in his attitude towards her that she knew exactly how he felt about her…or thought she did. But was there the merest glimmer of hope that…?

She checked the romantic thoughts that threatened to overwhelm her before they'd even had a chance to surface.

When the waiter had ushered them in she'd gathered that it was Carlos's favourite table. She couldn't help wondering how many elegant ladies he'd escorted here. The mysterious Maria, for example? Her name had been quietly mentioned by the man at the bar as they'd sipped their champagne. Sooner or later her curiosity would get the better of her and she would have to find out who she was. Perhaps Julia would know something about her.

The waiter was handing her a large menu that looked as if it might be a book on gastronomy if only she could translate the complicated Spanish. Pippa stared down at the first page before glancing over the top at Carlos.

'Would you like to order for me, Carlos? My Spanish is still a bit patchy where gastronomy is concerned, and I expect you know what to recommend at this restaurant.'

Carlos smiled. 'Is there any kind of food you really don't like?'

Pippa shook her head. 'I like everything, especially when someone else has cooked it.'

For their first course Carlos chose *gazpacho,* a cold cucumber and tomato soup made with oil and vinegar and flavoured with garlic.

'Delicious!' Pippa finished the last mouthful.

Plates were removed and a large dish of seafood paella was placed in the middle of the table. The waiter spooned some of it onto Pippa's plate.

She peeled the prawn that was sitting on the top of the beautifully presented dish, dipping her fingers into the lemon-scented finger bowl beside her plate.

'Mmm. I adore prawns, and these taste really fresh.'

He smiled. 'It's good to take out a lady who enjoys her food. It's no fun being with someone who picks at their food.'

Pippa put down her fork. 'That was the best meal I've had since long before Matthew was born.'

Carlos's eyes gleamed dark and mysterious in the candlelight as he leaned forward. 'That was only the starter. They're preparing a huge fish for us—ah, here it is! This was caught off the nearby coast this morning, so I hope you're still hungry, Pippa.'

The fish was so deliciously succulent that it seemed

to melt in her mouth and she enjoyed every last mouthful.

'I doubt if I can eat any dessert—' she began to say, but Carlos insisted she try a small *crema Catalana*. It turned out to be a kind of custard cream mould with a thin layer of caramel.

'A perfect end to a superb dinner,' Pippa said as she put down her spoon before adding, 'This really is the end of the meal, isn't it?'

Carlos grinned. 'If you can't eat any more it will have to be. Although once you get used to Spanish dinners you'll be able to pace yourself and take several more courses than we had tonight.'

Pippa sat back in her chair. She was still feeling out of place in this smart restaurant. She had so much to learn about this elegant way of life which the well-heeled clientele took for granted. But it was a way of life she could well get used to!

'We'll take our coffee out on the terrace,' Carlos was telling the waiter, before he moved around the table and stood behind her, his hands on the back of her chair, ready to escort her.

Pippa noticed that there was a gentle, very welcome breeze from the rolling plains surrounding the restaurant wafting over the terrace as she sank down into one of the comfortable armchairs beside a low table.

A waiter was hovering beside her chair. 'The *señora* would like a brandy with her coffee?'

Pippa declined, before turning to look at Carlos. 'Actually, I would have loved a small brandy to finish off such a superb meal, but I don't want to get Matthew drunk when I feed him tonight.'

Carlos laughed. 'Have a chocolate instead.' He held out a delicate china dish.

Their eyes met and Pippa felt a lurch of her heart. Careful, don't get carried away! Carlos is only being kind to a poor young single mum who is finding the first weeks of her baby's life a bit of a strain. Mustn't start reading anything more into it.

'Thank you so much for bringing me here tonight, Carlos,' she said quickly in a polite tone that was meant to indicate that she recognised that this situation was nothing more than a couple of friends on an evening out.

'It's my pleasure to be with you,' he said quietly.

She felt a small shiver running down her spine as she listened to his deep voice. His wide, sexy smile put her completely at ease. Looking at him now, he seemed so young and boyish.

'I'm intrigued as to how someone as young as you could become medical director,' she said, lightly.

Carlos laughed. 'I'm not all that young now. Thirty-two is a good age to be, but I think I know what you mean. The fact is I only came back here to please my father. I was fully involved with my work as a surgeon in Madrid. I had absolutely no intention of returning to my home village. But my mother died when I was young, my sisters are all married and busy with their young families, and my father's health was getting worse. He'd been diagnosed with lung cancer, so he begged me to come back home to live with him and work at the new hospital he'd built.'

'Your father built San Miguel hospital?' Pippa stared at Carlos in amazement.

He nodded. 'I don't mean he himself built the structure. My father was the doctor for this area, and when it became apparent that tourists and visitors were outnumbering the indigent population he decided we needed a hospital. From my grandfather he'd inherited a lot of land and a certain amount of money.'

He paused, leaning back in his chair as if warming to his subject. 'So he set the wheels in motion and created the hospital. It's partly under government funding now, of course.'

Pippa took another sip of coffee. 'Your grandfather must have been very rich.'

'He was a self-made man,' Carlos said proudly. 'He left school at an early age and started his working life with one small fishing boat—his inheritance from my great-grandfather, who had just died. Little by little he expanded his fleet before buying a small cruise liner from a bankrupt firm. This line of business flourished, so he expanded it. When he was seventy, he tired of always working, sold everything, bought a small cottage by the sea and spent the rest of his days fishing for pleasure.'

'He sounds like a great character.'

'Oh, he was,' Carlos said, fondly. 'As was my father.'

'I wonder if I ever met your father when I was down here as a child,' Pippa said. 'I remember spraining my ankle once and being taken to the local surgery to see the doctor. I remember he was tall…yes, very tall…and he was very kind to me. Beyond that I…'

'That would be my father. He was the only doctor around here for years. Where did you stay when you came down here?'

'On the campsite by the sea.'

'That's where the hospital is now. Maybe we met on the beach.'

'Perhaps we did,' She hesitated. 'Was it something of a wrench, leaving the bright lights of Madrid to come and take charge of a rural hospital?'

'It wasn't the bright lights I missed so much as the work interest. I loved my surgical work in Madrid and I didn't relish being an administrator. I made that quite clear to the interview panel. They assured me that if I was chosen I could run the place as I thought best. There were other candidates with similar qualifications and experience, but none who knew the people of this area as well as I do. I was born and bred here, and I used to go out on house visits with my father during my school holidays.'

'Your father must have been pleased when you got the job.'

'He was thrilled.' Carlos paused. 'I'm glad he lived long enough to see me installed here. Six months after that he died. I'd hoped that with the treatment he was having and the surgical operations he might live for another couple of years, but it wasn't to be.'

'I'm so sorry. That must have been a difficult time for you, starting up the hospital while still grieving for your father.'

Carlos's eyes held the veiled expression that Pippa had noticed before. He wasn't a man given to over-emotional displays of his feelings.

'Yes, it was difficult,' he said slowly. 'I also had to come to a decision. I'd taken the job of medical director to please my father. My original plan had been to stay until the end of my father's life and then go back to Madrid. But I found I had become too involved in my work here. I wanted to see the project through…so I stayed on. That was three years ago.'

'And you don't regret it?'

He shook his head. 'Absolutely not!'

He leaned across the table and took her hand in his. Pippa felt a shiver of excitement running down her spine as she looked into his expressive brown eyes.

'I have a wonderful life here in my birthplace, and I meet all sorts of interesting people. The life here is much calmer, far from the hustle and bustle of Madrid, and I have the time to get to know people. You, for instance. You wouldn't have come into my life if I'd been dashing back to the city. I would have delivered your baby on the plane and then I would never have seen you again, Pippa.'

Oh how she loved the deep, sensuous lilt of his accented English! She kept her fingers absolutely still as they lay in his gentle grasp, whilst deep down inside her fires were raging, causing havoc with her emotions. At that moment the chemistry between them was so highly charged that she felt there would be an explosion. Maybe there *was* hope that he didn't just regard her as a charity case…but she mustn't get carried away.

'I'll get the bill,' he murmured, removing his hand and beckoning to the waiter.

'I hope Matthew is all right,' Pippa said, when Carlos had settled the bill.

He was putting a leather wallet back into the inside pocket of his suit. He smiled as he stood up and came to hold out his hand towards her. 'Don't worry. Matthew will have been looked after for every second and proudly shown to everyone on the staff.'

*   *   *

It was only when they were nearing her apartment that Pippa began to wonder whether she should invite Carlos in for a drink. It was way after midnight, but she didn't feel in the least bit sleepy. Matthew had woken up when they'd put him in the car seat and was now making it quite plain that he wanted to be fed. Her breasts were also feeling terribly heavy, cramped inside her bra, so that would have to be her first priority on returning. Her mind was already jumping ahead to the possibility of feeding Matthew in the bedroom and leaving Carlos with his drink until she could put Matthew down in his cot.

The idea of feeding Matthew in front of Carlos didn't seem a good idea now. Although she'd felt no embarrassment at feeding on the ward, and knew that Carlos had been doing his rounds on at least a couple of those occasions, the situation seemed to have changed now. Yes, Carlos was a doctor, but she was no longer his patient in the hospital. She was now a colleague and a friend, but the highly charged atmosphere towards the end of their evening together meant that she wasn't sure how to handle her feelings towards Carlos any more.

The car had stopped and Matthew was now crying lustily. Pedro was already holding open her door.

'Would you like to come in for coffee, Carlos?'

There! She'd somehow plucked up the courage, but even to her own ears it sounded like a most improbable suggestion. Why would anyone want to follow her into her small, untidy apartment, wait until she'd fed her baby and all for a cup of coffee? Carlos was probably itching to get away, back to the ancestral home.

'Thank you for the kind offer, but the answer must be no. I have an early start in Theatre tomorrow…'

He glanced at the expensive gold watch on his wrist and smiled. 'I should say today. Some other time, perhaps.'

His head was bowed as he undid the straps on the baby seat, so Pippa couldn't see his expression, but she was sure it would be one of relief at being able to escape. He held the bawling Matthew briefly before handing him over to her.

'I think Matthew is trying to tell us that he's not only hungry but he needs his nappy changed.'

As she held Matthew against her the unmistakable aroma wafted up to her nostrils. She grinned as she saw the funny side of the situation. What a way to end such a romantic evening! As if to compound her return to the real world Carlos leaned across to her side of the car and patted Matthew's blond hair in a friendly but totally unromantic gesture.

He smiled. 'Goodnight, both of you.'

Both of you! That was the way he thought of them. A package that needed attending to. A couple of human beings he had to be nice to because they were far from home and family.

She took a deep breath as she realised she must banish such uncharitable thoughts. Carlos had given them a most enjoyable evening and it was she who'd invented the romantic ambience that she'd imagined had surrounded it.

'Goodnight, Carlos, and thank you so much for a wonderful evening.'

Clutching her screaming, smelly baby, she brushed past Pedro, still waiting by the side of the car. To her surprise Carlos now climbed out and hurried to her door.

'Give me your key, Pippa, so that I can open the door for you.'

'It's in my bag...'

He was opening up her capacious bag, still attached to her wrist, as she clung to her baby. He was oh, so close, but the thing foremost in her mind was the dirty nappy.

'Good thing you're a doctor,' she said, as he finally extricated her key and put it in the door.

He reached forward and placed his lips on her cheek. 'And I'm glad you're a nurse,' he said quietly.

Now what did he mean by that? She turned as she stood in the doorway, watching the sleek car pulling away down the cobbled street. After closing the door, she leaned against it. Even Matthew's cries weren't quite so loud for a few moments—maybe he sensed that his feed was imminent.

She shivered as she raised her hand to touch the place on her cheek where Carlos had rested his lips. Then with a determined effort she carried Matthew to the nearest chair so that she could pacify him. The nappy could wait until he'd stopped crying, because in the silent time that would follow she would be able to daydream and imagine the impossible.

As soon as her baby had latched on to her nipple peace and quiet descended, disturbed only by the contented suckling noise. She was free to start up a little story in her head, just as she'd used to do when she was a child. She would start it in the same way she always had done, with Once upon a time...

Once upon a time there was a wonderful, dishy, highly desirable man who met a young girl...fairly young woman...and asked her out to this flashy restaurant where she was totally overawed by the whole thing. But when they got back to her place she invited him in and he...

The sun was already high in the sky when she awoke next morning. Matthew was stirring in his cot beside her and she reached for him, wanting to reassure herself that all was well. He stared up at her with his big blue eyes and she was sure that his little mouth curved into a smile. She didn't hold with the theory that babies as young as this couldn't smile but were merely experiencing wind. Matthew had been smiling at her since the moment he was born, if only with his eyes.

'You're a happy little boy, aren't you, my darling?' she cooed. 'And you were a good boy last night when Mummy was enjoying herself with…'

The phone was ringing. Maybe Julia was phoning to say she was coming round to collect some more of her stuff. Pippa hoped so, because for some unknown reason she'd decided to move into the main bedroom herself, as soon as it could be cleared.

'Carlos!' Her heart leapt at the sound of his deep, sexy voice.

'Pippa, how are you this morning?'

'I'm fine!' Especially fine now you've called me!

'Not tired at all?'

'No, I had a good night. Carlos, thank you so much for a wonderful evening.'

'It was my pleasure, I assure you. Now, I'd better make this quick because I'm due in surgery again in a few minutes, so I haven't much time. Just taking a break between operations. But I thought you'd like to know that I've fixed it for you to start work mornings only in the maternity ward in three weeks' time. Bring Matthew with you and put him in the ward nursery, as we discussed. Julia knows all about the arrangement and will be very pleased to have you on her staff.'

Pippa could hear the murmur of voices in the background and the clanking of surgical equipment. She could picture him sprawled on a chair in the antetheatre, his theatre cap covering his dark hair. She tried to pull herself together and stop the romantic nonsense she was imagining. This was a professional gesture, nothing more.

'Thank you very much.'

'Make sure you get plenty of rest in the next three weeks. I'll give you my mobile number so that you can call me if you need my help. Anything at all that's worrying you, Pippa, please just pick up the phone. I'm switched off in hospital, of course, so I'll give you my hospital office number and my home number. OK? Here you are…'

Pippa grabbed a pencil and scribbled the numbers down. This was to be her lifeline, but how would she feel about phoning him? He was the medical director of the hospital, after all. Was this just a friendly gesture, the sort of situation you were in when you met someone on holiday and gave them your phone number, saying they must call you if they were ever in your area? And you knew there wasn't the remotest chance they'd take you up on it.

'Have you got that, Pippa?'

'Yes, thanks very much. But are you sure that…?'

'I'm absolutely sure that I want to help you, so give me a call if you need me.'

There was a great deal of warmth and animation in his voice as he said this. Pippa found herself smiling with happiness as she listened. In three weeks not only was she going back to her chosen profession, but she would also be coming into daily contact with Carlos. Life was looking very good.

'I've got to go now. Julia will call round to fill you in on the details. Goodbye, Pippa.'

'Carlos…' The line was already dead. So many things she'd wanted to ask him…

The phone rang again almost immediately.

'Hi, Pippa, it's Julia. How are you?'

'Fine. I'm feeling much stronger than the last time you saw me.'

'You sound great. What's happened?'

'Oh, nothing much. I've been able to get out more. and I'm getting used to being a mum.'

'Wouldn't be anything to do with Carlos Fernandez, by any chance? A little bird told me you'd been seen out with him.'

'News travels fast in these parts,' Pippa said as she heard Julia giggling down the line.

'Oh, only the usual hospital grapevine. Somebody saw you out at that posh restaurant over the hill. And then Carlos came on the ward early to inform me that you're coming in to work sooner than we expected. That's what I'm phoning about. I thought it would be easier if I called in to see you so I can answer all your questions. Will you be in this afternoon?'

'I'll make sure I am. And, Julia…could you take some more of your stuff away? I thought I might move into the bigger bedroom. Then Matthew can have the small one and…'

'Ah, I see!' More giggling.

'No, you don't, Julia! There's absolutely nothing going on.'

'If you say so, Pippa. Listen, I must dash. Got to get back on the ward…'

CHAPTER FIVE

WAS it really three weeks since that wonderful evening with Carlos? As Pippa looked down the ward from her vantage point beside the door she felt decidedly nervous at the prospect of meeting up with him again. During the intervening weeks she'd chosen not to call him because she'd found she was coping much better and she couldn't think of an excuse to ask for his help. He'd phoned her a couple of times to ask how she was, and of course she'd told him she was fine, and after a short chat that had been the end of that.

She'd hoped that Carlos might drop in one day, and when she'd been out in the village she'd found herself wishing that he would just turn up, as he'd done on the day he'd taken her to the restaurant.

But it hadn't happened. She'd just pushed the immaculate new pram that had been delivered to her door the day after their rendezvous with no note of explanation, and longed for the day when she could start work at the hospital. She'd sent a thank-you letter for the pram to Carlos at the hospital, as she didn't have his home address. It certainly wasn't the family pram he'd told her about, and she planned to ask him about it when she next saw him.

Looking at Carlos now, standing at the foot of a patient's bed with Julia and a couple of junior doctors in attendance, Pippa felt as if she didn't know him at all, as if that wonderful evening had simply been a figment of her imagination.

Julia glanced towards the door and beckoned Pippa to join them.

'Staff Nurse Norton is here, Dr Fernandez,' Pippa heard Julia say as she reached the bedside.

Carlos turned to looked at Pippa and smiled, his expression warm and friendly. 'Welcome back to the hospital, Pippa. Good to have you on board. How's Matthew? Is he settled in the nursery?'

'Yes, he's fine.'

'I've missed him. I'm looking forward to seeing him again. I expect he's grown.'

Pippa smiled. 'You won't recognise him. I've just fed him and he's gone to sleep in one of the cots.'

Carlos smiled back. 'I'll go and take a look at him when I've finished my round. So you're happy with the arrangement, Pippa?'

'Oh, absolutely!'

'Good.' Carlos turned his attention back to the patient. 'I believe you've met our patient, Melissa?'

Pippa smiled at the young girl who was lounging on the top of the cool white counterpane. The nail file poised in her hand made it quite clear that the visiting entourage was disturbing her manicure.

'Yes, Melissa had her baby the day before me. How are you, Melissa?'

Melissa pulled a face, put down her nail file and flicked her long blonde hair behind her ears.

'Bloody awful! I'm having problems with my boobs. You wouldn't believe how sore they are. I've had to give up feeding Anthony myself...thank God!'

Pippa experienced a wave of sympathy towards the young girl. It was obviously a case of mastitis, which was inflammation of the breast and could be very painful and distressing to the patient.

'Staff Nurse Pippa, perhaps you'd like to check on Melissa's breasts,' Julia said. 'I was going to do it myself but now that you're here I'll be able to carry on with my ward round. I know you've treated cases of mastitis on the maternity ward in your London hospital. I've set up a tray with the swabs and ointment required, and it's also time for Melissa's antibiotic medication.'

Julia gave Pippa a conspiratorial smile. The years had rolled away and they were both remembering a case in hospital soon after they'd finished their training. A young woman with a three-year-old toddler had come in complaining of sore breasts from feeding and when they'd asked where the baby was the mother had indicated the large fractious child chewing on a chocolate bar.

Pippa's face remained solemn. 'Yes, I've dealt with mastitis before, Sister.'

Carlos's arm briefly touched hers as he moved on. It was an accidental movement but she felt her breathing become more rapid. She was going to find it so hard to work alongside this man! Whether or not he chose to meet up with her off duty...well, the ball was in his court.

The medical entourage had dispersed. Pippa drew the curtains around the bed and leaned across her patient.

'Let me have a look at your sore breast, Melissa,' she said gently.

'You mean breasts, Staff Nurse. They've both gone bad. That's why they shoved me in here. What with you and my mum banging on about how I should keep feeding Anthony I just kept going, until some-body at the clinic noticed I was in trouble.'

Pippa leaned closer to examine the reddened, en-larged breasts, both nipples sore and encrusted. Areas on both breasts felt hard and hot to the touch. Glancing at Melissa's chart she saw, as she suspected, that her temperature and pulse were raised.

'Mmm, that looks painful, Melissa.'

'You'd better believe it! But I've never had a baby before so I thought I'd maybe got to suffer like this. Mum had told me it wasn't easy, so I didn't know what was normal, if you see what I mean.'

Pippa nodded. 'Now, I'm just going to swab the area here, near this nipple. It may sting a little at first but…OK?'

'No problem, so long as it's going to make me better. My mum keeps reminding me I'll have to help her when she gets back from hospital with her new baby.'

Pippa paused in mid-swab, holding her forceps in the air. 'Yes, you told me your mother was expecting a baby, but I didn't know it was so soon.'

'It's not for another month or so, but her blood pressure's sky-high so they've brought her in here. She's got two other kids, the twins, and this one on the way. Clive her husband's a randy so-and-so! Can't keep his hands off her. Disgusting at their age! That's why she said she wouldn't help me with my baby.'

'So where is your mum now, Melissa?' Pippa pat-ted the engorged nipple gently with a sterile swab and applied medicated cream to the affected area.

'Right next door, in the antenatal ward. What a laugh, isn't it? When she has her baby it'll be three generations all in the same hospital.'

'Who's looking after the other children?'

'My Anthony's here, and Clive, my mum's old man, has got the other two. Right little perishers they are, Jason and Rebecca. That'll cramp his golf handicap. Serve him right!… Ouch! Have you nearly finished, Nurse? Because I want to get on with my nails. One of them broke off when I was…'

Pippa listened politely to the endless chatter as she put her equipment back on the tray. She couldn't help feeling sorry for the girl. What kind of a life could she be having out here in a family where friction seemed to be the order of the day?

Later in the morning, she met up with Melissa's mother in the antenatal section. It was quite by chance that Julia had assigned her to check on the hourly blood pressure readings of this thirty-six-year old woman, and now, from her conversation with the patient, she realised that this must be Melissa's mother.

'Oh yes, that's my daughter,' the patient said. 'I love her to bits but we just don't get on. I was so worried when she phoned to tell me she was expecting a baby and wanted to come out here. With my third baby well on the way I just felt I wouldn't be able to cope, but she's my daughter so I couldn't put her off.'

Pippa nodded as she recorded the blood pressure reading on Penny Smithson's chart. 'I'm sure you've done everything you could to help your daughter, Mrs Smithson.'

Mrs. Smithson sighed. 'Oh, I don't know about that. I always felt I neglected her when she was little. I was only a child myself when I had her, just sixteen when she was born, so I had to leave school. I think

I resented her right from the start, although it wasn't her fault, poor little lamb. She didn't ask to be born.'

Pippa waited quietly. Her patient's blood pressure was too high and a gentle conversation would perhaps distract her. They weren't busy on the ward at the moment so she had time to listen.

'It must have been hard for you when you heard that Melissa was pregnant.'

'I was devastated. Talk about history repeating itself! But I wasn't surprised. She never knew her real father and Peter, the man I married after Melissa was born, couldn't have cared less what she did.'

She sighed again. 'I suppose you could say I shouldn't have left her back home, but I'd got a chance for a life at last, so I took it. My first husband is twenty years older than me. I only married him to get a bit of security for Melissa and me. But it was a big price to pay. I felt I'd lost my youth twice over. Peter and me didn't have any babies together, because he already had three kids from his first marriage and he said he didn't want to start all over again. He always found Melissa a bit of a pain, so...'

Pippa, although sympathetic towards her patient, began to think she ought to bring the conversation to a halt and report back to Julia. From what she'd heard it was obvious that both mother and daughter had had a difficult life.

'...so, as I say, I wasn't surprised when Melissa begged me to let her come out here. But I'd got used to just having Clive and me and our two little ones. It was like I was young again, and then my daughter turns up and suddenly I'm a grandma.'

'I can see you've had your share of problems,' Pippa said gently.

Studying her chart once more, she could see that the high blood pressure had been constant for some weeks. Mrs Smithson was being monitored to make sure she didn't suffer from pre-eclampsia, a dangerous condition which needed prompt action if the baby and mother's lives were not to be endangered. The maternity staff were on standby to deliver the baby if the blood pressure rose any higher, or any of the other symptoms of pre-eclampsia presented themselves.

The fair-haired woman leaned back against her pillows. She was only thirty-six, but Pippa thought she looked much older.

'Call me Penny. I'm not all that old, although I sometimes feel twice my age with all the worries. When I married Clive and came out here we thought we were in for a dream life. But two and a half kids later it's all gone a bit sour. I'm not even sure if Clive's going to stick by me. And then there's Melissa, with all her problems.'

Penny sighed deeply. 'Life never turns out as you expect it to, does it, Nurse?'

Pippa gave her patient a sympathetic smile. 'It certainly doesn't. Lean forward so I can do your pillows, Penny....There...that should make you more comfy.'

'You wait till you have kids. You won't know what's hit you...'

'I've got a baby—a lovely little boy,' Pippa said quietly.

The patient looked surprised. 'Doesn't your husband mind you working?'

'I'm on my own.'

'Really?' Penny looked thoughtful. 'Well, maybe you know a bit about what I'm going on about, then.

That's why you're such a good nurse. You've got experience of life.'

Pippa smiled. 'You could say that.'

Back at her apartment in the afternoon, Pippa kicked off her sandals and stretched out on the bed. She'd finally persuaded Julia to remove her belongings so that she could move into the main bedroom. Matthew now had his own little room, where Pippa had painted animals in a frieze around the room—ducks, cats, rabbits. She was looking forward to the time when she could teach him the names of the animals, but realised that by the time he could talk they would probably have moved on somewhere.

But where? Where was home now? Certainly not London. She could easily make this her home. She enjoyed the village life, the weekly market, watching the dancing in the village square near the church, trips down to the beach and to the harbour, pointing out the fishing boats to Matthew even though he didn't know what she was talking about. The rent on her apartment and the cost of living was very cheap compared with London. She could easily afford to stay on for as long as she wanted.

Oh, yes, she was settling in here. And San Miguel was where Carlos lived, so, in spite of herself, the place had a deep attraction for her. She didn't need a man to share her life with, but if the prospect of romance presented itself she would welcome it.

She leaned back on the pillows and gave a deep sigh as she realised she was being totally unrealistic. Carlos was way beyond her! The sort of life he was used to, the kind of people he mixed with…

And what did she have to offer him? A single mum who…

The phone was ringing. When she heard Carlos's voice at the other end she couldn't believe the coincidence. It was almost as if by wishing for him she'd made him call her. She was on the point of saying she'd been thinking about him at that moment, but managed to check herself just in time as she listened to him courteously asking how she'd got on during her first morning at work.

'I enjoyed it very much,' she said, responding in the same polite manner.

'I went in and looked at Matthew, but he was asleep so it seemed a shame to wake him. He looks in excellent health. I'll be able to spend more time with him next time he's here.'

'He slept most of the morning, until it was time for me to take him home.'

'Good, then we can expect to see you at work again tomorrow?'

'Of course.'

She waited, but there was no sound from the other end. Was it her place to end the conversation now? Was he still there?

'Carlos?'

'Actually, I was wondering if you would like to go to the village festival on Sunday. I know you're trying to find out about the culture and life of this area, so I think you would enjoy it.'

'I'd love to.' Was he intending to go with her, or…?

'Good. I'll pick you up at noon.'

'What about Matthew?'

He sounded surprised by the question. 'What about

Matthew? I don't suppose he'll want to join in the dancing but he'll enjoy the music.'

It was a good thing Pippa had been extremely busy during the week, because she could hardly wait for Sunday to come. At noon exactly she opened the door to let Carlos into her apartment. One thing she'd noticed about her medical director: he was meticulous in his punctuality and expected all his staff to be the same.

She'd spent the morning cleaning the apartment so that the place would look good when he arrived. Fresh flowers in the living room gave off their scent and she'd mopped the kitchen floor, even cleaned some of the windows. Now, through the open windows could be heard the hum of voices and the beginning of the festival music down the street near the church.

'I've left the car round the corner. Pedro will stay beside it until we need him. I'll carry Matthew because the pram isn't practicable in a crowd.'

'Talking of the pram—did this pram really belong to one of your sisters?'

He gave her a boyish grin. 'When I examined the one I had at the house I decided it wasn't smart enough for Matthew. So I chose another one…'

'That was very generous of you.'

'Not at all.' Carlos bent down and lifted Matthew from his pram. 'Only the best will do for a special boy like Matthew.'

Pippa felt her heart leap with happiness at the sight of this wonderful man holding her child. 'He's nearly two months old now,' she said proudly. 'And I'm beginning to distinguish all his different sounds. He's got his own little language already.'

'I'm sure he has,' Carlos said solemnly, looking down at Pippa, a serious expression on his face. 'That's because he's talking to his mother and she understands what he's trying to say.'

'I can't wait until he begins to talk properly! I've got a theory that babies begin by uttering an "mm" sound because that's the shape of their mouth when they first begin to suckle. Soon this becomes ma-ma and...'

She broke off. 'I don't want to bore you with my theory. It's just I find it so fascinating now that I've got my own baby and...'

'I can see that, and I love your enthusiasm, Pippa.'

His voice was sending shivers of longing down her spine. She found herself fantasising about what life would be like if Carlos were the father of her child. Just suppose the three of them were a family unit, setting off to the festival together, a whole lifetime of love and laughter ahead of them...

Matthew began to wriggle and Carlos put him over his shoulder, gently stroking his back.

'Where do you intend to be when Matthew says his first word, Pippa?'

She took a deep breath. 'I've no idea. My contract lasts until October, as you know. After that...who knows?'

'Are you planning to join Matthew's father, perhaps?' Carlos asked quietly.

'Absolutely not! Ian will be able to see Matthew whenever he chooses to come and see him, but that part of my life is a closed book...for ever.'

'For ever is a long time. You may change your mind.'

Pippa shook her head vigorously. 'No chance!'

There was a short silence which neither of them broke as each seemed deep in thoughts of their own. Pippa hoped she had made it quite clear to Carlos that she was a free woman, so that if there was any chance of her impossible dream coming true...

'Let's go to the fiesta!' Carlos raised Matthew above his head.

Matthew gave a little chuckle of delight and a dribble of milk splashed down onto Carlos's immaculate white shirt.

Carlos laughed as Pippa grabbed a tissue and began to sponge the offending mark away.

'Don't worry, Pippa! On fiesta day it doesn't matter how you look. Unless one is a beautiful girl like yourself. Today you are looking enchanting, *señorita!*'

'*Gracias, señor!*'

She smiled up into his eyes, her heart pounding. Carlos's tone had been light, not to be taken seriously, but she was glad she'd taken time out at the end of her cleaning session to shower and change into the new cotton skirt and blouse she'd bought in the village. The assistant had assured her that the bright scarlet blouse would look good with her blonde hair, and the mid-calf length white skirt was very flattering.

As they walked down the street Pippa felt very proud of her beautiful baby and the handsome man holding him. They looked like the ideal family, but as Carlos was so well known in the village she knew that nobody would be taken in by appearances. She sensed that some of the glances their way were curious.

Who's the girl our doctor is with? Where's the father of the baby? Pippa could almost read the questions on everybody's mind. Carlos didn't seem to worry at all, and chatted briefly to everyone who stopped him in the crowded street. Pippa could still only understand a smattering of these conversations. Twice she heard the name Maria—the mysterious Maria that she still didn't know anything about and hadn't dared to ask for fear she might hear something she didn't want to.

The music was growing louder in the square. People in colourful costumes were holding hands, forming a circle and dancing gracefully together.

'This dance is called the *sardana*,' Carlos told her, raising his voice to make himself heard above the haunting sound of the music.

The people drew back to the side of the square at the end of the vivid dance, making way for a troupe of dancers in red, white and black costumes to perform in the middle of the crowd.

'These are the Castells,' Carlos said. 'As you can see they're beginning to form a human pyramid.'

'It looks incredibly dangerous,' Pippa said, as she watched the men nimbly climbing onto each other's shoulders.

A couple of young boys from the troupe leapt upwards with agile limbs and formed the final peak of the pyramid amid ecstatic applause from the crowd.

Pippa clapped her hands. 'That is just so spectacular!'

Matthew chose that moment to start wailing.

'Spectacular or not, Matthew's had enough,' Carlos said, edging his way through the crowd. 'Are you OK behind me, Pippa?'

'I'm fine! Just keep going.'

Carlos waited for her at the edge of the square.

Matthew was now screaming loudly in protest at the noise and the hunger pangs in his tummy.

'Maybe I should take him home,' Pippa said. 'I'll have to feed him and…'

'You can feed him in the café. We need our lunch too.'

Somehow she found she'd lost her shyness as she unbuttoned her blouse and guided Matthew's little rosebud mouth to her breast. Carlos had chosen a table in the corner of the café and nobody batted an eyelid at the sight of a young mum feeding her baby. And as for her expected embarrassment at feeding in front of Carlos—it had completely disappeared.

Carlos poured her a glass of wine. 'It's a very light wine. Very little alcohol content. Nursing mothers in this part of the world have been drinking it since the beginning of time.'

Pippa smiled. 'You talked me into it.'

She stretched one hand towards the table, but Matthew wriggled and she had to make him comfortable again with both hands. Carlos smiled as he picked up her glass and held it to her lips. She was very thirsty so she took a large gulp, which made her splutter and some of the wine spill onto Carlos's shirt.

Carlos grinned. 'Not only does the baby mess my shirt, but the mother is trying her best to ruin it too.'

Pippa giggled as the wine fizzed up her nose. 'I'm so sorry. When I've finished feeding I'll find a tissue.'

Carlos was laughing. 'I'll take you back to my house after lunch, so we can all clean ourselves up. It's so hot I think we need a swim. We'll call in to your apartment and you can pick up a swimsuit. Unless you have something else planned, of course…'

'I'd love a swim.'

She checked her naive question about him having a pool. All the smart houses around here had them, especially the well-established ancestral homes.

Matthew fell asleep soon after Pippa had finished feeding him. Carefully she lowered him onto the bench seat beside her, packing him round with cushions so that he wouldn't fall off.

They ate a simple salad of anchovies, olives, tomatoes and endives, followed by fresh fruit. In her mind Pippa was already deciding which swimsuit she would wear. Down on the beach she always wore her black swimsuit, to make her feel safe and respectable. But in the safety of a private home she would perhaps dare to be seen in one of her new bikinis.

What on earth had possessed her to buy such risqué garments she couldn't imagine! But a couple of days ago, in the same little boutique where she'd bought her lovely skirt and blouse, she'd seen these tiny scraps of fabric, one white, one black, and had simply felt the bikinis were right for her. She hadn't been able to choose between them, so she'd bought them both. At the back of her mind had she somehow envisaged that she might get a chance to swim with someone who really mattered?

'You're looking very thoughtful all of a sudden.' Carlos's voice interrupted her thoughts as she chewed the last morsel of a succulent peach.

Pippa smiled. 'Just thinking about this afternoon. It will be nice to have a swim rather than simply splash in the sea. When I go down to the beach I carry Matthew into the water with me, but it's not the same as being able to actually move around a bit.'

'You'll be able to swim as much as you want. Matthew and I can play football together at the side of the pool.' Carlos was looking around him, raising his hand to attract the attention of a waiter so that he could settle the bill.

'*Camero—mi cuenta, por favor.*'

Pippa gathered Matthew into her arms as Carlos paid the bill. Her baby snuggled against her, his little body warm and relaxed, totally trusting her every movement. Did he have any idea that he was in the hands of a first-time mum with no experience of babies outside of hospital? A mum who wasn't sure what was going to happen in the immediate future, let alone in the years to come.

Carlos was moving the table so that she could get out more easily. She followed him to the door. The fans in the café had cooled the air, but outside the afternoon sun was very hot. Carlos took baby Matthew from her and they headed off up the street towards her apartment.

It was a relief when they were finally able to get inside the cool, air-conditioned interior of the car. It had been hot inside her apartment, with all the windows closed, and it hadn't been worth opening them during the brief time it had taken to pack a couple of bikinis and some things for Matthew into a bag.

Pedro had been running the air-conditioning in the car for a few minutes in preparation for their departure. Pippa sank back against the luxurious seat in the back of the car. Matthew, beside her in the car seat, kicked his little toes furiously and gurgled happily. Carlos had chosen to sit beside Pedro and was talking animatedly to his driver in rapid Spanish. He turned for a moment and playfully tweaked Matthew's bare foot. Matthew gurgled more loudly and gave his approximation of a lopsided but bewitching smile.

Pippa closed her eyes. It was such bliss to be with a man she could trust like this. She felt instinctively that he was an honest man, that if ever they formed a serious relationship she wouldn't have to worry that he would start to two-time her.

She opened her eyes quickly as romantic thoughts poured through her mind. She was leading herself into dire trouble if she continued thinking like this. Yes, she might be falling in love with Carlos, but love was probably the last thing on his mind when he took her out with Matthew. It was obvious he loved babies, and he was a kind, dutiful person who wanted to make sure everyone was happy and well cared for. She could dream all she liked but she couldn't change that.

Carlos's house was spectacularly impressive. As the car purred up the gravel drive Pippa caught her breath. From the stone façade, with its crenellated rooftop, down to the tall stone pillars that divided the front terrace into shaded alcoves, everything about the place denoted wealth and understated opulence.

'I know what you're thinking, Pippa,' Carlos said as Pedro brought the car to a halt at the front of the house.

For heaven's sake, she hoped not! 'So, what am I thinking?'

'You're thinking like everybody does when they come here for the first time. This is the house of a very rich man. That was exactly what my grandfather first planned. When he became rich, at the end of a lifetime of hard work, he had this place built to impress. I remember when I was very small, sitting with him in a small boat out on the sea, and he told me that when he was young he struggled hard to get rid of the image that he was only a poor fisherman.'

Carlos leaned over the back of his seat, his eyes shining as he recounted his story, and Pippa sat forward in her seat listening, spellbound, enjoying the fascinating sound of his deep, charmingly accented voice.

'And then, when he became rich, he had this house built as a status symbol so that everyone would know how successful he was. But he told me that the older he got, the wiser he became. He realised that money and possessions couldn't make you happy. So as soon as my father got married my grandfather gave him everything and moved back to the small cottage near the harbour where he had been born. His life had turned full circle and he was happy again.'

'What a lovely story,' she breathed. 'I would have liked to meet your grandfather.'

'And he would have liked to meet you,' Carlos said softly, reaching out to take her hand in his.

The touch of his fingers was deeply unnerving. She looked into the dark expressive eyes so near to her now and had to suppress a shiver of excitement. Whatever the future held, she hoped that Carlos would be a part of it.

'Maybe I did see your grandfather out there on the sea when I was a child,' she said quietly.

Carlos nodded. 'He was still taking his boat out every day when he was well into his eighties, so you probably did... Come on, let's go inside.'

It was cool inside. Walking through to the terrace at the back of the house, Pippa caught a fleeting impression of paintings on the walls, high ornate ceilings, antique ornaments, intricately woven carpets and large vases of fresh, heavily scented flowers standing on the polished surfaces of the opulent furniture.

She was unable to suppress her admiration for the place. 'I absolutely love this house!'

Carlos, carrying Matthew, stopped and put one hand on her shoulder. 'And I'm sure the house loves you already.'

Her heart began to pound. She felt as if she was coming home—and that was a dangerous feeling to have in these delicate circumstances. Carlos was leading the way once more, out to a cool, shady terrace overlooking a large garden bedecked with flowers, shrubs and shady trees. Overhead fans whirred softly in the background, competing with the sound of the cicadas in the garden. Water sprinklers played on to the parched lawn which led down to a large swimming pool, shining blue and inviting in the afternoon sun.

'Que quieres beber, señora?'

Now seated in a cushioned wicker armchair, Pippa smiled as she looked up at the elderly lady who had just asked her what she would like to drink. Dressed from head to toe in black, she gave the appearance of being someone who had served the family for many years.

'Would you like fruit juice, Pippa?' Carlos put in, as he saw her hesitating, unsure of what was on offer.

'Yes, please.'

From the interior of the house a phone was ringing, The lady in black disappeared inside, to emerge seconds later requesting that Carlos go to the phone. Apparently it was Maria.

Pippa held her breath. For some reason she'd begun to dislike this woman with the name Maria, whoever she was…and, more importantly, whatever she meant to Carlos.

CHAPTER SIX

PIPPA waited on the terrace for Carlos to return. From
the adjoining room she could hear his voice, animatedly talking in rapid Spanish, occasionally laughing
at something the mysterious Maria had said. She tried
to tell herself that it was silly to be jealous of someone
she'd never met, especially when she herself meant
nothing to Carlos. But there was an awful niggling
feeling at the back of her mind that Maria was bad
news.

The lady in black, who Carlos had introduced as
Señora Montejo, brought a jug of iced fruit juice, setting it down on a table before indicating that she
wanted to take the baby to a cooler place indoors. In
a mixture of the *Señora*'s broken English and Pippa's
limited Spanish it was agreed that Matthew would
sleep better inside, where there was a family nursery.
Pippa was assured that the *Señora* would stay with
the baby in the nursery, as she always had done with
the children of Carlos's sisters.

Matthew slept on as he was transferred from the
arms of his mother to the kindly lady who whispered
soothing words to him as she carried him away.

Carlos returned from his phone call. 'I saw Señora
Montejo taking Matthew to the nursery. You don't
need to worry about him. Our wonderful housekeeper
has looked after all the Fernandez children. She used
to take care of me, especially after my mother died,
and she's the most caring person I've ever met. She

96

considers herself a housekeeper here, but she's part of the family now. When I was a child it was just like having a second mother.'

'I can see she's a natural with babies,' Pippa said. She hesitated. 'It was lucky that you were at home to take your phone call.'

Carlos sat down in the chair beside her, running a hand nonchalantly through his thick dark hair.

'Oh, Maria would have called back, or got me on my mobile,' he said casually.

'Is Maria one of your sisters?'

Pippa was trying not to sound too inquisitive, knowing quite well that Maria wasn't one of the names Carlos had mentioned when he'd discussed his four sisters with her on their first evening together at the restaurant.

Carlos's dark eyes flickered but his expression gave nothing away. 'No, Maria is just an old friend. We go back a long way.'

Pippa hoped he meant old as in ancient, much older than himself! But a gut feeling told her that was wishful thinking.

Carlos placed the glass of fruit juice in front of her. Thoughtfully, she took a sip, leaning back against the cushions. They sat together in amicable silence for a few minutes, looking out across the garden. A couple of slender, colourful dragonflies were playfully weaving themselves in and out of the exotic flowerbeds.

Pippa finished her drink and put the glass down on the table. 'It's so peaceful here.'

Carlos gave her a lazy smile. 'Not even the sound of a crying baby. Talking of which, we'd better have our swim now, before Matthew wakes up and you have to feed him again. Come on, bring your bag and you can change by the pool. We used to have swimming parties when I was a child, so my father had some changing rooms built.'

The white multi-arched building which housed the changing rooms blended in well with the surroundings. It was even marked 'Señores and Señoras' so Pippa needn't have worried about being embarrassed when she changed into her bikini. She decided on the white bikini for this first appearance.

Glancing at herself in the full-length mirror, she was glad she'd managed to acquire a light tan. Her figure wasn't what she would like at the moment, but it would sort itself out when she'd finished breast-feeding. At the moment she looked top heavy! Large breasts above a narrow waist, and, apart from a little extra flab on her tummy, the rest of her too thin by comparison. Oh, well, it was a small price to pay for the miracle of producing her darling little Matthew.

She left her sunglasses on the changing room table and emerged blinking into the bright sunlight.

'*Caramba!* You look *magnifico, señorita!*'

Carlos came towards her, his arms outstretched. For one breathtaking moment she thought he was going to take her in his arms and kiss her. But it was merely his Mediterranean way of demonstrating appreciation. Looking at him now, she felt her skin tingling with excitement. The black swimming shorts moulded to his body left nothing to the imagination…and her imagination was running away with her at the sight of his athletic, muscular body.

They swam together, side by side, until she tired after a few lengths, returned to the shallow end and walked up the marble steps at the edge of the pool. She covered one of the sunbeds with the large, fluffy white towel she'd brought out from the changing room and lay back, her eyes closed, to recover from her exertions. It was ages since she'd had the opportunity to swim like that and she felt quite whacked.

She also needed to check on the state of her breasts! Now, nearing another feed-time, they were feeling heavy; with a surreptitious hand she made sure she wasn't leaking milk. She reassured herself that she was OK. She could relax and enjoy herself for a few more minutes.

Carlos came out of the pool, running his hands through his dark hair as he pulled up a sunbed and joined her.

She turned to look at him, stretched out beside her, and felt the now familiar longing feelings which came on whenever she was close to him.

'It's very kind of you to bring me here, Carlos,' she said quietly.

'Kind!' He sat up abruptly and she stared at him in alarm. 'I'm not being kind, Pippa. I'm doing this because…because I really care about you. And I feel happy when I'm with you.'

He leaned across and put a long finger under her chin, tilting it so that she was staring up into his eyes.

'Don't ever think I'm simply being kind. Believe me, I wouldn't spend time with you if I didn't want to. I don't know what it is about you, but…'

He pulled her against him, gently caressing the side of her cheek with long, sensitive fingers, and then he kissed her. She sighed as she felt his hot lips claiming hers. Was this a dream, or was it happening for real? She didn't know and she didn't care. The tumultuous churning of her emotions had become a maelstrom of wild desire. She was a flower opening up to the welcome rains after a long dry spell in the desert.

She felt him shift his weight on to her sunbed and she curled her body against his, her skin tingling erotically as it made contact with his. He kissed her again, his lips light at first but then firming as his kiss deepened. As she gave herself up to his caressing hands she realised that she wanted him to take her completely. The passions he was arousing inside her could only be satisfied by the ultimate consummation.

They would take it slowly… She would enjoy his teasingly caressing hands, as she was doing now, before she gave herself completely to this wild feeling of abandon that was claiming all her senses…

But even as the thought crossed her mind she felt a shred of normality entering her consciousness, disrupting the heavenly experience she longed to continue sharing.

They couldn't make love here, where they might be disturbed…

She stirred in Carlos's arms and with an effort pulled herself away. Carlos immediately moved back on to the other sunbed. From a sitting position he looked down at her with a troubled expression.

'I'm sorry, Pippa. I shouldn't have got carried away like that. You are a guest at my house and…'

'Carlos, we both wanted it, didn't we? I wasn't fighting you off, was I?'

She surprised herself with her boldness. For the first time since she'd met Carlos she felt that she was the one in charge of a situation, that it was up to her to make the right decision.

She sat up, pushing her damp blonde hair behind her ears. 'The timing was wrong, that's all. I was afraid Señora Montejo might arrive with Matthew for his feed and...'

Carlos's eyes flickered. 'And I was afraid that I was being...oh, how do you say it in English?...presumptuous, forward, impetuous? I don't think that really describes how I felt when this longing feeling came over me. What I mean to say is that perhaps it was too soon because you hardly know me...'

'Carlos, to be truthful I feel as if I've known you all my life.'

He leaned across and kissed her gently on the lips. As he drew away there was the sound of a telephone ringing in one of the changing rooms. Carlos leapt to his feet and disappeared inside. When he emerged he was smiling.

'You were right about Matthew being ready for a feed. Señora Montejo thinks the baby is hungry and requests that you go to the nursery.'

Pippa smiled back as she stood up. 'I'd better get dressed.'

They sat on the terrace together in the twilight, watching the sun dipping down into the sea beyond the edge of the garden. The sun had become a fiery ball as it slipped ever lower down in the sky. Pippa, holding Matthew in her arms, gave a sigh as it disappeared into the water.

'On holiday I was always so sad when the sun disappeared,' she said wistfully. 'My brother and I used to wander down to the beach out there in the early evening and watch the sun. It meant our day was over and we were supposed to go back to the tent. But we often stayed on to look at the bright colours in the sky...there, you see!...the pink and orange glow blending in with the darkening of the sky.'

Matthew had closed his little eyes and was sleeping peacefully. His final feed of the day would be much later, but she felt she ought to make her way home soon.

'I think I should be going home soon.'

'Why? What do you have to do that's so pressingly urgent?'

'Well... I...'

The phone was ringing again.

'Excuse me, Pippa.' Carlos went inside.

Pippa could hear his low, urgent voice. He emerged, frowning.

'I have to go back to the hospital. There's an emergency in the maternity ward, and as it's Sunday evening, which is usually quiet, we only have a skeleton staff in. I'm supposed to be off for the entire weekend, but as medical director I can never be truly off duty.'

He was already moving away, but he turned to look down at her. 'Please stay until I get back. Señora Montejo will take care of you, and when I return we can have supper together.'

Hearing her name, the kindly housekeeper came out onto the terrace, speaking rapidly to Carlos. He replied quickly, obviously giving some instructions, before moving off down the terrace.

'Carlos!' Pippa stood up and moved quickly to catch up with him. 'If Señora Montejo is happy to take care of Matthew I'd like to help you at the hospital. I've had a lot of experience in obstetrics. I know that Julia is off duty this weekend, so...'

Carlos turned to look at his housekeeper, who was

already making it clear she understood and that Matthew would be safe with her.

'Yes, come with me, Pippa,' Carlos said briskly. 'I think you will be very useful.'

'What's the problem in maternity?' Pippa asked as Carlos drove quickly down the drive and turned out through the wrought-iron gates.

'It's Penny Smithson, our prenatal patient with high blood pressure. Do you remember her, Pippa?'

'Of course. She's the mother of Melissa, our patient suffering from mastitis.'

Carlos nodded as he turned the wheel quickly to avoid a large stone in the narrow private road, left behind by a road-mending crew.

'That's right. The staff nurse in charge of the maternity ward tonight is concerned that Penny's blood pressure is getting higher each time she checks it. Our consultant obstetrician is away for the weekend, so I have to stand in for him if there's an emergency. When I've found out how serious the condition is I'll come to a decision about the baby. Obviously we would prefer Penny to go to full term, but it may be too dangerous to wait so long.'

They reached the hospital and Pippa called briefly into the staff cloakroom so that she could change into one of her white uniform dresses. Carlos was already on the ward when she arrived. Sofia, the young Spanish staff nurse in charge of the ward, was looking worried as she stood beside him. Whilst Carlos examined their patient, Sofia explained to Pippa what had happened since she'd been on duty last Friday morning.

Pippa felt her concern mounting as she heard that

this evening not only had Penny complained of seeing flashing lights in front of her eyes, but she had developed a severe headache. To add to these problems, the nurse who'd tested the patient's urine had reported that traces of protein were detected, another sign that Penny's condition was worsening.

These three symptoms were cardinal signs that the patient was now suffering from the condition known as pre-eclampsia. Both the mother and the baby were in danger. The rapid pulse-rate of the unborn baby showed that it was already suffering distress. It would have to be induced, or removed by surgical intervention.

Carlos straightened up from his examination and took off his sterile gloves as he looked down at the patient.

'We're going to take you down to Theatre, Penny,' he said gently. 'I'm going to deliver your baby by Caesarean section, which means that...'

'I know what that means, Doctor,' Penny said, between sobs that sent tears trickling from underneath the lids of her closed eyes. 'I don't care what you do so long as you get rid of this foul headache. My head feels as if it's going to burst open.'

She opened her eyes, wincing at the pain. 'But you'll make sure my baby's born OK, won't you? I couldn't bear it if something happened to this one.'

Carlos patted her hand gently. 'We'll do all we can. Don't you worry.'

He turned away from his patient. 'I'll set up the theatre,' he told Pippa and Sofia quietly. 'Emergency pre-op preparation here, and then Staff Nurse Norton will join me in Theatre.'

'What's going on?' Penny's daughter Melissa

pushed through the curtains and stood by her mother's bedside. 'Mum, what's the matter?'

On his way out, Carlos paused for a second to put his hand on Melissa's arm, but she shrugged him off.

'Your mother needs peace and quiet, Melissa.' Carlos looked across at Pippa. 'Take over, will you? I must get down to Theatre.'

'Peace and quiet, my eye!' Melissa said, leaning over her mother. 'Mum, what have they done to you? You look awful!'

'Thank you, darling.' Penny dabbed a hand over her red weeping eyes. 'You always did know exactly what to say to make me feel better.'

Pippa reached across and wiped Penny's face with a tissue. 'Your mother is going to go down to Theatre for a Caesarean shortly, Melissa. There's a problem with her blood pressure so it's best we deliver the baby tonight.'

'Oh, Mum!' Melissa flung herself dramatically on the bed. 'I didn't know you were really ill. I just thought you'd come in here for a rest, to get away from the kids. I'm sorry I said all those awful things about you. Mum, I do love you, really…you're not going to die, are you…?'

Pippa put an arm round Melissa's shoulders and gently but firmly pulled her off the bed. 'Come on, Melissa. I'll take you back to your own bed so that your mother can get some rest before her operation. She's in good hands and we'll do everything we can…'

Glancing back at Penny, she saw that her patient had now composed herself and was resigned to whatever was going to happen to her. 'You're going to be fine,' she told her.

Penny passed a hand over her eyes. 'God, I hope so! It was bad enough with the other two, but this time…'

'I'll give the premedication,' Sofia told Pippa. 'When you've settled Melissa you'd better get down to Theatre.'

Pippa stripped in a cubicle in the ante-theatre and put on a theatre gown and cap. Inside the main theatre she put on sterile gloves and walked over to the operating table. Carlos was standing across the table from the theatre sister, a small dark-haired Spanish woman of an indeterminate age. Pippa had seen her before in the hospital and had formed the opinion that she looked confident and experienced. She was the sort of nursing sister who would have terrified her during her days as a raw recruit in the preliminary nursing school! But now, several years on, with qualifications and experience under her belt, Pippa felt relieved to have someone like that as a colleague.

Sister turned to look at Pippa and her eyes held a friendly expression above the mask. She indicated that she wanted Pippa to stand beside her. Pippa took her place, glancing across the table at Carlos. She could tell that beneath his mask he was smiling. His confidence in her, asking her to assist this evening, did wonders for her morale. She was a member of a valuable team once more.

The anaesthetised patient was wheeled in and settled on the table. Carlos murmured briefly to the anaesthetist at the head of the table before making the first incision. Pippa watched as Carlos cut through the abdominal wall, making an incision in the lower segment of the uterus. There was only one other nurse, very young, very junior and obviously inexperienced in the theatre, so it was Pippa who had to act as runner for both Sister and Carlos. She was kept busy, organising a steady flow of sterile instruments and instructing the junior where to place the discarded, now unsterile instruments.

The tension in the theatre was palpable as the minutes passed, and then suddenly Pippa heard a wailing cry as Carlos lifted the tiny baby out through the abdominal wall. It was always a relief when the baby cried immediately. Especially now, when they'd been so worried that the baby might have suffered too much distress in the womb before they could get her out.

Yes, it was a little girl. A perfectly formed little girl. This was the moment when Pippa felt a great surge of happiness that she'd been able to play a part in bringing a new human being safely into the world. But they weren't out of the woods yet. This tiny little infant would probably need extra intensive nursing care.

The junior nurse had tears in her eyes.

'Is this your first operation?' Pippa asked her quietly.

The nurse nodded. 'I'm so scared of Sister,' she whispered. 'I'm glad you came along to show me what to do. It's been wonderful, seeing the baby born like that.'

Sister was handing Pippa the baby so that together they could start the postnatal checks. Pippa cleansed the tiny nostrils and inserted a narrow tube so that she could administer some oxygen

Carlos came across to check on the baby himself.

'It's obvious there's some immaturity of the lungs,

but otherwise we have a healthy baby,' Carlos said. 'Thank you, Sister, and Staff Nurse.' He turned to look at the young nurse. 'And thank you, Nurse, for your help.'

The young nurse turned bright pink and Pippa smiled. Carlos seemed to have that effect on his female staff.

Pippa settled the baby in an incubator and wheeled her through into the special care area of the nursery. The staff nurse in charge took over from her.

'When Penny Smithson comes round from the anaesthetic and is fully conscious she can be wheeled in to see her,' Carlos said, coming up behind her. 'But only for a short time. I'll be here in the morning, to see how mother and baby are doing. If you're worried you can reach me on my home number.'

He turned to look at Pippa. 'I think you and I have a little debriefing to do, Staff Nurse.'

On the journey back to the house above the sea Pippa remained quiet. The emergency operation had taken her mind off her own personal problems, but now they all came rushing back. If she'd gone home at the end of her swim this afternoon she would have avoided having to make decisions about how far she wanted her relationship with Carlos to go.

But oh, then she would have missed those tender moments by the pool. And she was glad that she'd been able to assist him this evening. But everything was moving so fast. She hadn't imagined this morning, when they'd set out to the fiesta, that they were to be anything more than friends and colleagues. Their relationship had changed so much during this one day they'd spent together.

'You're very quiet, Pippa. Something worrying you?'

They'd reached the rough part of the road to the house and Pippa could see that Carlos was concentrating on his driving, hands gripping the wheel, eyes scanning the dark road illuminated by the headlights.

'Nothing's worrying me,' she said quickly. 'I...I'm simply tired, that's all.'

'And hungry, I'm sure—because I'm starving. Señora Montejo will have supper ready for us when we get home. I telephoned her from the hospital to say we were on our way.'

Pippa swallowed hard. This was the point at which she'd planned to pick up Matthew and say her goodbyes. But it wasn't as simple as that. Life never was. She'd experienced so much happiness today, but she had a sneaking feeling it couldn't last.

This sense of euphoria. The beginning of a new relationship... But how would it all end? Really, she didn't know enough about Carlos to go ahead with a whirlwind romance, did she? She knew nothing about other relationships in his life apart from the mysterious Maria, but there must be masses of women out there for him. Or maybe Maria was the one particular woman who just didn't happen to be here at the moment. That would be even worse.

As they drew up in front of the house, passing the spotlights discreetly hidden at the sides of the drive to light up the impressive façade, she was trying to think of a way of politely thanking Carlos and Señora Montejo, picking up Matthew and phoning for a taxi. It would be simpler all round. Later, when she'd learned more about Carlos, and if she still felt he was attracted to her, she would know how to handle the situation.

It was incredible that she should be so hesitant! She'd lain awake at nights thinking about Carlos ever since she'd met him. She'd had dreams about him, for heaven's sake! Dreams at night and daydreams, when she'd fantasised about what would happen if...

And now, when he was showing a definite interest in her, she was getting cold feet—making excuses as to why she couldn't go along with this unbelievable feeling of rapport that had sprung up between them...

He stopped the car and the touch of his fingers on her bare arm sent a frisson of excitement running through her whole body. That was the trouble with physical contact with a man like Carlos. He could send all sensible mundane thoughts from your mind by the merest touch of his hand.

'What is it?' He put out his arms and gently pulled her towards him.

In spite of her resolve, she melted against him. 'I was just wondering if I ought to take Matthew home now. It's late and...'

He smiled, looking down at her with an enquiring but infinitely tender expression.

'Pippa, Matthew doesn't care where he is, so long as his nappy isn't too soggy and he gets fed and cuddled at regular intervals. I'm not going to take you home until you've got a good meal inside you.'

He held her at arm's length again and she felt reassured. He was planning to take her home after the meal. There wouldn't be any complications. She wouldn't be put in a position where her treacherous body would take off into heavenly outer space and pull her emotions and weak resolutions along with it.

He opened his door and went round to her side to let her out. She looked up into his dark, handsome face as he held the car door open for her. There was nothing to be frightened of in this situation but her own impossible desires. If she could keep a check on her emotions then she was sure that the situation would be easy to handle.

Señora Montejo was waiting for them in the large entrance hall. She told Pippa that baby Matthew was still asleep, advising her to eat supper before he wakened up for his last feed of the day.

'Thank you so much for taking care of Matthew, Señora Montejo,' Pippa said. 'I'll just take a peep at him before we have supper. I know he's sleeping, but it seems so long since I've seen him. I'm not used to being away from him.'

The *señora* smiled and led the way to the nursery. Matthew was lying on his back, one chubby little arm flung up behind his head, one lying on the white cotton cover.

'He looks like a little angel,' Señora Montejo said in Spanish, before hurrying away to finish the preparations for supper.

Pippa smiled as she put out her hand to smooth back the wisps of blond hair from his little forehead. There was a movement behind her. She turned, not having realised that Carlos was with her.

'He's a fine-looking boy,' he said quietly.

With a perfectly natural movement he rested one hand on her shoulder. She remained absolutely still, revelling in the closeness of him yet willing herself to remain detached and uninvolved.

Impossible! She was already in thrall to his charisma. And why should she fight this feeling simply because she thought it was too precious to last? Why torture herself when the simplest way would be to go along into the uncertainty of the unknown?

She turned away, not realising she'd given a big sigh.

Carlos was instantly concerned about her. 'Are you OK, Pippa?'

She smiled up at him. 'I'm fine.'

'Well, then, let's go down for supper.'

Sitting at the polished mahogany table in the ornate dining room, being served with home-made soup by the indefatigable housekeeper and knowing that everything was under control as far as Matthew was concerned made Pippa feel infinitely cosseted. She felt very much at home here.

She smiled at Carlos. 'I'm glad you talked me into having supper. I hadn't realised I was so hungry.'

'It's not a good idea to start worrying unnecessarily on an empty stomach. Problems often disappear after a good meal.'

His eyes held an enigmatic expression when he looked at her.

Pippa heard the closing of the door behind her as Señora Montejo went out of the dining room. Looking at Carlos now, his eyes so tender and full of understanding, she realised that he'd probably surmised what was worrying her. He was a highly sensitive man and he must be having doubts about their relationship himself. They'd met in such strange circumstances and known each other for such a short time.

Suddenly she knew that it was going to be all right between them.

Better than all right! That was such a tame description of the way she felt about being with Carlos. She felt sure he was a man who could be trusted, so why not enjoy what was ahead? But it was Carlos who would have to indicate that he was ready for a relationship first...

After finishing their soup, they helped themselves to cold meats, salad and fruit laid out on a side table.

'Señora Montejo has gone to bed,' Carlos said, carving a slice from the joint of roast ham and serving Pippa with a piece. 'She has asked me to tell you that she made up the bed in the small room adjacent to the nursery. She thought you might be too tired to make the journey home tonight.'

Pippa's mind was working at a brisk rate as she returned to the dining table and put the plate down on her tablemat. Carlos, close behind her, resumed his seat at the head of the long table. Pippa was seated on his right. She looked down the table, wondering about the people who'd sat here in the past. It was an ornate, expensive table, but obviously well used by the family. And being invited to stay the night like this by the housekeeper made her feel as if she was part of this family.

She reasoned that there would be no harm in sleeping in a small room within earshot of baby Matthew.

'Staying the night here with Matthew in the nursery would seem to make sense,' she said slowly. 'Of course I would have to leave early in the morning, to get back home and prepare for work.'

Her voice sounded so prim and proper, even to her own ears. But she was trying to set parameters, to make sure she didn't get carried away. She needed to go slowly, to feel her way into this complicated, unexpected but infinitely exciting and unpredictable relationship.

Carlos smiled. 'I know what you're trying to say, Pippa.'

Pippa's expression gave nothing away. 'Do you? I doubt it, because I'm not sure myself.'

She put down her knife and fork and looked at Carlos, a deep sense of bewilderment overcoming her.

He put out a hand and covered hers. 'Stop worrying. We often have guests to stay in the house. It's all perfectly proper.'

A loud cry came from the direction of the nursery up above. Pippa was relieved that something had broken the tension of the moment. 'I think Matthew is trying to tell me he's ready for his supper.'

Carlos rose from his chair. 'Finish your own supper first, Pippa. First rule of motherhood. Look after yourself for the sake of your baby.' He turned at the door. 'I'll bring Matthew down and we can take turns holding him while we finish eating.'

Carlos returned from the nursery, cradling Matthew. He was snuffling around, but calm at the moment, expecting that he would soon be fed.

Pippa held up her hands towards Carlos and the baby. The sight of Matthew in Carlos's arms was unnerving her. They looked so right together. Her darling baby, the centre of her life, and this man who was rapidly stealing her heart.

'Let me hold Matthew first,' Pippa said, taking the baby in the crook of her arm and continuing to eat her supper with a fork in her other hand.

Matthew's initial reaction to being put on hold was

noisy. He grizzled for a while, and then began screaming.

Carlos stood up. 'Here, let me take him.'

The screaming continued as Carlos walked around the room, stroking Matthew's back, talking soothingly to him, telling him that Mummy must have her supper first. And then, as if some magic wand had been waved, he started to listen to what Carlos was saying and calmed down. It was as if he understood what was going on and was prepared to wait.

'You've certainly got a way with babies,' Pippa said as she put down her knife and fork. 'I'll take Matthew up to the nursery and feed him now. He's been very patient.'

'Would you like me to bring you a cup of coffee, Pippa?' Carlos asked as he handed over the baby.

Matthew gave a loud yell as he was disturbed once more.

'No coffee, thank you. It keeps me awake if I drink it late at night. But if you have some camomile tea…?'

Carlos smiled. 'Of course.'

Pippa settled herself into a specially designed low nursing chair. The cushioned upholstery of the chair was well worn and it was the most perfectly comfortable chair for breastfeeding. She wondered how many Fernandez babies had been nursed in this chair. Matthew latched on vigorously and suckled noisily.

'You were a hungry baby, weren't you, darling? No wonder you were making all that noise. And Mummy had left you for ages and ages, hadn't she? Poor little lamb. Whatever was Mummy thinking about, leaving her little treasure to…?'

She continued whispering quietly to Matthew as she fed him. Fondly imagining that he was listening to her meaningless chatter, she noticed that his eyes were closed and knew that all he really wanted was something to fill his little tummy and take away that empty feeling. She was so busily concentrating on her baby that she didn't hear Carlos coming into the room. The first she knew of his presence was when a cup of camomile tea appeared on the side table.

She looked up and smiled at Carlos. He sat down easily in a chair, not too far away, placing a cup of coffee and a glass of brandy beside him.

'I'm not disturbing you, am I?' he asked gently.

'Not at all.' She hesitated. 'I've been wondering how many babies have been fed in this chair.'

Carlos gave her a long slow smile. 'I couldn't give you an accurate number. Let me see…'

He frowned in concentration. 'All of my four sisters, and then I was the fifth baby in my generation to be nursed there. I remember when I was about six I started jumping up and down on the chair and my mother came into the nursery to remonstrate. She explained that it was a very old and precious chair.'

Pippa settled herself more comfortably, feeling honoured that she should be sitting in it. 'Something of a family heirloom, then?'

Carlos nodded. 'My grandfather gave it to my mother on the day she told him she was going to have her first baby. It had belonged to his mother and he'd collected it from the tiny cottage down by the harbour. And then all the visiting babies and my sisters' children have used it. It's been re-upholstered a few times, I believe, but I'm surprised it's lasted as long as this.'

'You'll no doubt use it for your own children, I'm sure.'

She looked down at baby Matthew, aware of an annoying flush spreading over her cheeks.

'I expect I will,' he said, his voice husky with emotion.

'Were you spoiled as a child?' Pippa asked quickly. 'I mean, being the only son after four daughters.'

'Never really thought about it. Yes, I suppose I was. My sisters used to tease me and try to boss me around, but I could always get my own way. I think it's a good idea to have sisters—you understand women better when you grow up.'

She laughed. 'Ah, so you think you're an expert on women, do you?'

He gave her a rakish grin, standing up suddenly to cross the room and sit beside her on the nearest chair, his body almost touching hers.

'I like to think so. For instance, I can usually tell what women are thinking when I'm with them.'

'And what am I thinking now?' she asked facetiously, turning her face to look into his eyes, which were dangerously close to hers.

'You're thinking how much you'd like to finish feeding Matthew so that you can relax at the end of your long day.'

His voice was deep and husky, sending shivers of anticipation down her spine. This was the feeling she'd vowed to quell as soon as it arose, but something inside her was asking why she shouldn't go along with it.

She hesitated. 'Not quite. Try again.'

'You're thinking about what you'll do when Matthew falls asleep. Trying to decide whether you'll persuade me to drive you home or whether you'll simply enjoy the rest of the evening with me.'

'Partially true,' she said, still maintaining the same light tone.

'Well, it looks like our little cherub is well satisfied now, so why don't you put him down in the cot and let me help you come to the right decision.'

Our little cherub, not *your* little cherub, Carlos had said. A slip of the tongue, perhaps, but it had affected her deeply. In her present mood, the closeness between them was palpable. It was as if the three of them had formed a family unit…or was she being impossibly romantic about the situation?'

She put Matthew over her shoulder, willing him to burp quickly. Never had she been so pleased to hear the resounding sound that meant she could lay him down again.

Carlos was standing behind her, his hands lightly holding her waist as she lowered Matthew into his cot and tucked the counterpane gently around him. Her body was alive with the possibilities of the night that stretched ahead of her and as she turned around Carlos took her in his arms.

She sighed as she moulded herself against his hard, muscular body. 'I think I'd like to stay here.'

'And I think you've made the right decision, Pippa,' Carlos said. 'I'm glad you're not going home, but that doesn't mean we have to spend the night together. I shall respect your wishes if you prefer to…'

'Shh!' She placed one finger against his lips. 'I want to be with you tonight, Carlos…'

His eyes searched her face. 'You're absolutely sure?'

She could feel her body reacting to his concern for her. Her mind was telling her that Carlos was someone who could be trusted.

Slowly, he bent his head and kissed her, gently at first, and then with a greater intensity of feeling. A feeling of total abandon crept over her. The real world had ceased to exist and she was beginning to float away on cloud nine...

Pippa stretched her arms langourously as she surveyed the ceiling of the master bedroom, her whole body still vibrant from their ecstatic lovemaking. She had only a vague recollection of how she'd got here. She'd been so fired up with desire as Carlos carried her across from the nursery that she hadn't noticed anything.

She didn't want to put on the bedside lamp, but by the light of the moon streaming in through the open casement windows she could distinguish the basic outline of the large room and its furnishings. Huge floor-to-ceiling cupboards dominated one wall, and there were some bookshelves near the bed. Open windows claimed the whole of the wall she could make out most clearly in the moonlight, and she noticed that there was some sort of balcony or terrace outside which was accessed by French windows.

The perfect place for breakfast in the morning sun! No, she didn't dare stay so long. But she wouldn't think about the morning just yet. She turned to look at Carlos and felt a frisson of desire rekindling itself.

He was sleeping soundly, his head almost touching hers. She moved carefully so as not to waken him. She must go and check on Matthew. They'd left the door of the nursery open; that much she did remember. And the nursery was only just across the corridor, so she would have heard any sound that Matthew made.

Her baby was sleeping peacefully. He'd kicked off his light cotton cover but it was a warm night so it didn't matter. Carlos had told her there were no mosquitoes in this area, so Matthew was quite safe. The San Miguel town council had a rigid plan for exterminating the insects which was working extremely well. All stagnant water had been drained or treated, and constant spraying of the area had shown good results. She stayed for a few moments looking down at him, undecided about whether to go to her own bed in the little adjacent room or...

'Pippa!'

Her heart gave a little bound of happiness as she heard Carlos calling for her in that quiet, husky, tantalising voice. The decision had been made for her.

As she went back into the bedroom Carlos sat up, swinging his legs over the side of the bed. He strode towards her, his arms outstretched, and she thought how even more handsome he looked when he was completely naked. There was not a shred of embarrassment between them now. They'd crossed the frontier that divided friends from lovers and it was the most wonderful feeling.

'Come back to bed,' he whispered, gently pulling her against him.

'I woke up and went to check on Matthew.'

'How is he?'

'He's fine. I would have wakened if he'd cried out, but I wanted to make absolutely sure.'

For a few moments, as they stood entwined in each other's arms, Pippa thought how strange it was to be in the middle of a romantic liaison and to be keeping one ear open for any sounds from her baby. But as Carlos lifted her onto the bed all thoughts of Matthew disappeared. She was a young carefree girl again, with the most wonderful lover in the world…

This time their lovemaking was slow and unhurried—Carlos deliberately teasing, tantalising, driving her wild with desire and longing, so that when he finally entered her she felt a great surge of emotional release. And as her whole body climaxed again…and again…and again…she cried out in orgasmic ecstasy…

CHAPTER SEVEN

IT WAS very early morning when Pippa slipped out of bed again. She moved cautiously towards the bedroom door and crossed the landing to the nursery.

She looked down at her baby's calm, peaceful features, feeling a great surge of love. He looked as if his little rosebud mouth was smiling in his sleep. That could be more her imagination than anything else, but she wanted to feel that he was happy too. Happy to be here in this warm, welcoming house.

Turning away, she tiptoed into the little adjacent room and climbed into the single bed. Snuggling down under the cotton sheet she realised that she'd never felt so happy in her life. She had everything she'd ever dreamed of. A wonderful baby and the man of her dreams.

Not so fast! The still small voice of reason sent a cold shiver down her spine. She mustn't be too proprietorial about Carlos. Just because they'd spent the night locked in each other's arms, experiencing the most ecstatic lovemaking in a totally out of this world experience, it didn't mean that this state of affairs would continue into the far distant future.

They were lovers, yes. But how long it would last she had no idea. She didn't even know whether she would be invited here again. This might simply be a one-off experience.

She sat up and rearranged her pillow before lying down again. No, she was being unduly pessimistic.

Carlos wouldn't have been so infinitely tender and romantic with her if she was simply a one-night stand. He was an honourable man. But she mustn't take anything for granted.

That was why she'd come here, to her designated bed, so that she could wake up on her own. Later on she would possibly have to come face to face with Carlos at the hospital in his role of medical director. So she would have to distance herself from the events of the night…if that were possible!

Her disturbing thoughts began to quieten and she slipped into an uneasy sleep, only to be wakened shortly afterwards by the sound of Matthew crying. Time to get back into the real world and leave her dreams and fantasies behind.

'So how was your weekend, Pippa?' Julia looked up from the case notes she was studying in her office as Pippa walked in.

'Oh…' Pippa hesitated, searching for some way of describing her fabulous weekend without giving too much away. 'Very interesting. I took Matthew down to the village to watch the fiesta.'

'I hear it was very good. Would you like a coffee before you start work? I've just made a fresh pot.'

'Yes, please. I need something to kickstart my brain.'

'As good as that, was it?' Julia said in a knowing voice, reaching over her desk for the coffee pot and another cup.

'You mean my weekend?' Pippa asked in an innocent don't-know-what-you're-talking-about type of voice.

'Come off it, Pippa! We've known each other long

enough to recognise when one of us is trying to play it cool and being hopelessly unsuccessful. You may not have had time to put on any make-up this morning, but, looking like the cat that got the cream, you don't need it! Who is he?'

'Julia, why do you always assume that there has to be a man involved if—'

Pippa broke off as the door opened and Carlos walked in. A slow pink flush crept over her face. She didn't dare to look at Julia. Maybe her friend would think it wildly improbable that the latest recruit to her staff on the maternity ward had spent the weekend with the medical director, but then again…

'Buenos dias.' Carlos moved across to Julia's desk.

'Coffee, Carlos?'

'Yes, please. I need something to wake me up this morning.'

He was trying to stifle a yawn. Pippa raised her eyes and saw that he was watching her. Only the tender expression in his eyes revealed that he was remembering the wonderful experiences they'd shared together.

When he'd dropped her off at her apartment this morning they had both been trying to make the transition from ardent lovers to professional colleagues. Pippa knew that their weekend together had to be kept secret.

He drank deeply from the cup, as if he was parched with thirst. 'I've come in to have a look at Penny Smithson. Our obstetric consultant will be in later this morning. I've already filled him in on the details of the case over the phone, but I thought I should see her myself.'

'I was surprised when Night Sister gave me her

report to hear that you were the one who performed her Caesarean, Carlos,' Julia said.

'It was essential to act quickly,' Carlos said. 'How is Señora Smithson this morning?'

'Night Sister has just told me that she's had a reasonably comfortable night, helped by the sedatives you prescribed. I'll take you along when you've finished your coffee.'

Julia turned to look at Pippa, who was struggling to hang on to her regained composure.

'If you'd like to come along with us, Pippa, you could help Mrs Smithson. I'm told the baby has been bottle-fed during the night, but we need to get the mother's colostrum flowing. You've had experience of post-operative Caesarean patients, haven't you?'

Carlos drained his coffee and put down his cup. Julia and Pippa followed him out through the door, down past the antenatal section and into the postnatal section of the ward. Penny Smithson was lying flat, her hair spread out over the pillow, her face strained with anxiety. Beside her, sitting on a chair, her daughter Melissa, their mastitis patient, was keeping up an endless flow of chatter.

'Mum, you're going to be OK. I'll help you all I can when we both get out of here. I'm younger than you, and when they clear up this trouble with my boobs...Oh, hello, Staff Nurse Pippa. It was nice of you to look after me last night. I was so scared when you took Mum up to Theatre, but look at her now! And have you seen my beautiful little sister? Well, half-sister, she is, I suppose. I've been along to peep through the glass.'

'Were you here last night, Pippa?' Julia asked quietly.

'Yes, I came in to help out. They were short-staffed.'

The unanswered question about how she had happened to find out she was needed was left unanswered for the moment. But Pippa knew that Julia wouldn't leave it at that. Sooner or later she would have to explain everything—well, not everything. She would hold back as much as she could.

Carlos moved nearer to the bed and Julia asked Melissa if she'd mind going back to her own bed for a few minutes.

'Staff Nurse will be along soon to treat your breasts,' Julia added, before turning her attention to their post-Caesarean patient. Before she could speak to her about being examined by the doctor, Penny Smithson had put out her hand and taken hold of Pippa's.

'Thanks for everything last night, Nurse,' Penny said warmly. 'I was in such a state when you first arrived, but you were so kind to me. Were you in the theatre when I had my op?'

Pippa nodded, aware of Julia's eyes on her. 'Yes, I was there.'

'And it was you who took baby Rosemary out, wasn't it, Doctor? I can't thank you enough. She's going to be all right, isn't she? They wheeled me along to have a look at her early this morning, but she seems so small. She's very beautiful, a bit like my Melissa was when she was born, but so tiny.'

'Perhaps you'd like to help Dr Fernandez with his examination, Staff Nurse?' Julia put in quickly. 'You both seem to know more about this case than I do. Having just come on duty after my weekend away, I've only got the information that the night staff have given me, so if you'll excuse me I'll catch up with my other patients.'

Julia's voice was totally professional, but Pippa could tell that she was annoyed that she hadn't been put in the picture. Pippa busied herself with preparing Penny for Carlos's examination. With the sheet rolled back, she surrounded the operation area with sterile dressing sheets. The abdominal scar looked healthy enough, but their patient complained she had difficulty finding a comfortable position.

'At this early stage it is always difficult,' Pippa said in a sympathetic tone as Carlos stripped off his sterile gloves. 'For the time being you'll find it helps if you rest on your side with your arms around a pillow…like this.'

'Yes, that does feel better,' Penny said, easing her body into a more relaxed position. 'Now, when am I going to start feeding Rosemary? With my other babies I always got to feed them immediately, so what's the problem with this one?'

'It's too early for Rosemary to start suckling,' Pippa said gently. 'Being slightly premature, she's very tiny, and she needs some help with her breathing because her lungs are a little bit immature. For the moment we're keeping her in an incubator to help her. In a few days she'll be strong enough for you to feed yourself.'

'Yes, but what's she feeding from at the moment?'

'She's being nourished with a special formula but she'll shortly be able to take the breast. I'll bring along a pump and you can express. That will keep your milk flowing, and also we'll be able to give it to your baby when she's strong enough to suckle.'

She glanced up at Carlos, who was looking down at her in approval.

'Staff Nurse is absolutely right,' he said solemnly. 'She's had a great deal of experience of premature babies.'

Penny smiled. 'I feel more relaxed now I've seen you both. Do you think you could tell Melissa I'm going to have a little nap? We're getting on really well now—the best we've been since she was a little child. But she never stops talking and I could do with a rest.'

Pippa smiled back at her patient. 'I'm glad you two are good friends again. I'll ask Melissa to give you some time to yourself, explain that you need lots of rest at the moment.'

Carlos remained by her side as they walked down the ward, his hands by his sides—oh, so close, but careful not to touch. She had the distinct impression that it must be blatantly obvious to all the patients that they'd spent the night together. She was so deeply conscious of the movement of his body beside hers, that faint aroma of the aftershave she'd seen in his bathroom.

Everything about them must surely proclaim that they were more than colleagues. It simply wasn't possible to shrug off that deep awareness of each other, but she had to try. The last thing she wanted was to cause professional problems in this hospital for either herself or Carlos.

He paused by the swing doors. 'Thank you, Staff Nurse. You've been most helpful,' he said quietly.

Looking up at him now, she saw that he was trying desperately to suppress an amused smile. She wondered if the whole ward could see the chemistry that was flowing between them. Momentarily, he bent his head and whispered.

'I'll call you this afternoon. Will you be at home?'

She nodded, and his smile broadened before he went out. Turning back into the ward, she saw that Julia had been watching them, no doubt putting two and two together. Julia, her dear, dear friend, was no fool!

As she set off back down the ward she knew she would have to tell Julia what was going on. She owed it to her friend. If it hadn't been for Julia she would never have come out here, never have met the most fantastic man in the world—never have begun to piece together a life that had been in danger of falling apart.

Pippa paused at the bed where Julia was advising one of the patients on how to feed her new baby. Holding the baby against the new mother's breast, she kept her eyes firmly on the patient, apparently unaware that Pippa was there.

'I'll fill you in later, Sister,' Pippa said.

Julia looked up and gave Pippa a conspiratorial smile as she moved to the foot of the bed. 'I should hope so, Staff Nurse.'

'The information will be strictly confidential,' Pippa added quietly.

'Of course.' Julia hesitated. 'How about this evening?'

Pippa frowned, remembering Carlos had said he would phone her. If he was feeling as she did, they would surely meet up this evening. 'I'll have to let you know. I may be busy.'

Julia raised her eyebrows. 'As bad as that, is it?'

Pippa gave her a wry grin. 'Or as good. Whichever way you like to look at it.'

Carlos phoned during the afternoon to say that one of his sisters was having a birthday dinner that evening. He'd forgotten all about it until he looked in his diary. Pippa dried her hands on a teatowel, wiping the phone at the same time. She'd been in the middle of handwashing a pile of clothes, her own and baby Matthew's. There was no such thing as a washing machine in this apartment, so she'd resorted to soaking everything in soapy water in the sink and then rinsing it out in clean water.

It was a tedious, boring process, so she'd been excited when she'd heard the phone ringing, expecting it to be Carlos coming up with some wonderful idea for the evening.

She tried to hide her disappointment. 'Well, of course you must go.'

'I could call in on the way back, Pippa, but it will probably be very late.'

'Not a good idea. I need to have a long sleep tonight.'

His sexy chuckle echoed down the line. 'Me too. I'm feeling exhausted already...' Slight hesitation. 'But you were worth it...'

She took a deep breath, not knowing whether to speak or wait for Carlos to continue. What could she say? That she'd never been so happy? Somehow she couldn't find the right words. An innate feeling of caution was holding her back.

When he began speaking again his tone was much brisker, more matter-of-fact.

'I'll call you at the weekend. I'm going up to Madrid tomorrow, for a medical conference.'

'Fine, I'll be here.'

She hesitated, unsure whether to change her mind about tonight and tell Carlos that it didn't matter what time he called in after his sister's birthday dinner. Being with Carlos was more important than sleep... But something was holding her back, telling her to play it cool, not to be too available. The fact that they wouldn't see each other again until the weekend would only add spice to their eventual meeting.

She cut the connection before ringing Julia on the ward.

'So where is lover-boy tonight?' Julia asked as she stretched herself along the sunbed on the apartment terrace.

The plastic sunbeds covered in squashy cushions were the best place to relax in the evening when it was cool. During the day it was too hot, but after sundown, with Matthew settled in his cot, it was the perfect place for a quiet read.

Pippa, relaxing on the other sunbed, heard Julia referring to Carlos as lover-boy and smiled nervously. 'Was it so obvious this morning?'

She'd filled Julia in on the barest details of her weekend and sworn her to secrecy. But she knew that Julia, being Julia, would want to know more.

'Carlos had to go to a birthday dinner for one of his sisters. He's got four sisters, you know.'

'No, I didn't know,' Julia said dryly. 'You're obviously well in. But not so well in that Carlos wanted to take you to meet his sisters.'

Pippa felt a cold hand clutching at her heart. 'Why

should he? We've only known each other a few weeks…'

'Quite!'

Pippa looked across at her friend. 'What are you trying to tell me, Julia?'

Julia drew in her breath. 'I don't want to be a kill-joy, Pippa, but Carlos is from a completely different culture to you. Out here in this part of Spain they do things differently. His family…well…his family is all-important to him. I don't know how serious he is about this affair you seem to have started together, but I would hate to see you hurt. I feel responsible for uprooting you and bringing you out here, so…'

'Look, hang on a minute.' Pippa stared at Julia. 'Get to the point. If you've got something important to say, then…'

Julia was frowning as she sat up. 'I don't want you to get carried away by the idea that this is a romance that could last. As I say, you and I are different from the people out here. I'm already having doubts about my own affair with Pablo Rodriguez. I suspect he's cooling off, and…'

'Look, don't imagine that your affair is remotely like mine!' Pippa flung at her. 'Carlos and I, well—'

She broke off in embarrassment as she saw the worried look on her friend's face.

'You can never be sure,' Julia said carefully. 'One thing I do remember Pablo telling me some time ago, when we were discussing Carlos, was…' She paused and looked carefully at Pippa, as if searching for the right words.

'Go on—don't stop now.' Pippa said. 'But first I'd like to know why you were discussing Carlos with Pablo.'

Now it was Julia's turn to look embarrassed. 'Well, it was actually when I remarked to Pablo that it seemed strange that a good-looking man like Carlos from a strong family background wasn't already married. Pablo told me there's some woman in Madrid who seems to have some kind of hold on him, that they've known each other a long time and there have been a lot of unconfirmed rumours about a relationship between them.'

Pippa held her breath as a cold wind seemed to blow over her. Could this be Maria? She looked out across the small garden, illuminated in the moonlight—the same moon that had shone last night through the open casement windows of Carlos's bedroom. How different the moonlight seemed tonight.

'Pippa, are you listening to me? I'm only telling you what Pablo said, and all I'm advising is that you tread carefully. Don't get carried away. After all, it isn't so long since you were let down by Ian—and now you've got Matthew to think about. I mean, for heaven's sake, don't imagine you're falling in love with the man.'

Too late! Pippa drew in her breath as she tried to look composed. What was the recipe for falling out of love? But she didn't want to. This was only Julia being ultra-cautious. But, coupled with her own mounting misgivings about her precarious situation, her relationship with Carlos now seemed very fragile.

'Thanks, Julia. I promise not to rush into anything stupid.'

But hadn't she committed herself already? Hadn't she worshipped Carlos with her body last night and he with his? Or so she'd thought. What did Julia know about real love? Maybe about as much as she did, she admitted to herself grudgingly. They were neither of them experts on the subject.

'We're both experts on making mistakes where men are concerned, aren't we, Julia?' Pippa said in a small voice.

Julia laughed. 'That's more like it. Once you can see the funny side of things and don't take yourself too seriously, you'll survive. I'm going to help myself to some more of this excellent wine. Sure you won't join me? Just one glass?'

'Better not. Got another feed coming up soon.'

Julia hauled herself off the sunbed. 'Tell you what, I'll make you some camomile tea. Live dangerously, my girl. It's just like old times, isn't it?'

Not quite, Pippa admitted to herself, but at least she would have a shoulder to cry on if everything went sour.

For the rest of the week she threw herself into her work on the ward, finding blessed release from worrying about Carlos when she was fully occupied. In the afternoons she made a point of taking Matthew out in his pram. There was usually a sea breeze on the beach, and she parked the pram under the trees before strolling down to the water's edge for a paddle.

Talking to Matthew about how he would soon be able to paddle and then swim gave her a sense that she wasn't lonely. But as she found herself longing for the weekend she began to doubt whether Carlos would phone. While he was away in Madrid he might decide to cool it. She hoped he really was at a conference, and not simply meeting up with the woman Julia had mentioned.

*   *   *

There was no phone call on Saturday. She'd had no contact with Carlos all week. He would have phoned by now if he was keen to see her again. She lay on her sunbed on the terrace during the evening, reading a book that had gripped her at the beginning but now, with her eyes constantly glancing over at the phone, couldn't hold her concentration. She climbed off the sunbed, closed the windows and went into her bedroom.

When sleep finally claimed her it was only for her to dream that she was rushing out into the sea, getting into difficulties, screaming out that she was drowning…

She woke up, realising that her screams were little more than deep moans. She was bathed in sweat, her breathing rapid and irregular. Climbing off the bed, she went into the next room to see if she'd disturbed Matthew. He was lying on his back, a light snoring sound coming from his mouth.

She smiled. He looked so angelic. At least she would always have her son with her. Her own flesh and blood. Whatever happened she'd been given this miraculous gift of life. Matthew and she were a real family. They didn't need anyone else…did they?

She went back to bed and read her book until it became light again. She got up, then went into the kitchen and made some tea. It was still early. She would have time for a shower before Matthew needed feeding.

The hot water cascading over her hair was soothing and refreshing at the same time. Fumbling for her towel, she stepped out of the shower and began to plan her day. She'd finished the chores yesterday, so she could devote the whole day to Matthew. They would go down to the harbour to see the boats, and then...

She froze at the sound of the phone. Who would call her this early? Dear God, she hoped it wasn't Ian. With the time difference in America he often phoned at unsocial times. But most recently she'd hoped he'd got the message that she wanted his calls to stop unless it was something that concerned Matthew. Simply begging her to go over to the States to be with him was most unwelcome and futile.

She wrapped the towel around her wet body and padded back into the kitchen, rubbing her hands on the towel to dry them.

'I hope I didn't wake you, Pippa.'

Her heart gave a little hop, skip and a jump at the sound of Carlos's voice.

'Carlos, where are you?'

'I'm at home. Got back late last night. I just woke up and, remembering that you're an early riser, I thought I'd give you a call. What are you doing today?'

It was as if he'd never been away! She forgot that he hadn't contacted her, that he might have been meeting some mysterious woman, that she'd felt totally neglected and had practically written off the idea of ever going out with him again.

'I haven't made any plans,' she said quickly, ashamed that she was so blatantly available to him.

After all the warnings Julia had given her she should have been more cool, but she couldn't help herself. Relief was flooding through her.

'Would you like to come and spend the day here?'

She tried to curb her enthusiasm. 'Yes, that would be...very pleasant.'

'Good. Pedro will drive down and collect you. Can you be ready in about an hour?'

'I think so. I can hear Matthew waking up, so when I've bathed and fed him I'll get myself ready.'

'Breakfast will be ready when you arrive. *Hasta la vista!*'

Carlos came out of the house to help her from the car and carry Matthew.

'I do believe you've grown, Matthew.' Carlos held her baby at arm's length while he studied him.

Turning to Pippa, he leaned down and kissed her gently on the cheek. Something in their relationship had changed since he'd been away. The passion of the previous weekend was missing, possibly dormant, and Pippa couldn't decide whether it was a good sign or not to have reached the stage where she liked having a peck on the cheek.

Following Carlos into the cool interior of the house, she told herself she was being unreasonable. She would have liked Carlos to take her in his arms, tell her he'd missed her, reassure her that there was no other woman waiting in the wings… But how could he, with the baby in his arms? She was being unduly critical simply because she was feeling very insecure.

She remembered Julia's words. *Don't imagine you're falling in love. I'd hate to see you hurt.* She made a mental note to remain as detached as she could today. Yes, she would enjoy herself, enjoy seeing the loving bond develop between Carlos and Matthew. But she was going to keep a tight rein on her emotions. And tonight she would go home to her own bed.

They had breakfast on the terrace with a beautiful view of the gardens. The bread and flaky rolls tasted home-made, or they might have come from one of the excellent bakeries in the area. As she looked across the small table towards Carlos, Pippa could feel her heart contracting with emotion again. It was so wonderful to be here again in this house which, although far more opulent than any house she'd ever lived in, somehow felt like home.

Señora Montejo seemed to accept Pippa as part of the family, and her happiness at seeing Matthew again was a joy to witness. She'd claimed the baby as her own responsibility, and soon after Pippa and Matthew had arrived the *Señora* had taken him with her to the nursery.

Carlos and Pippa swam later in the morning. The water in the pool was already warmed by the sun.

'There's no need for heating during the summer,' Carlos said as they swam together side by side. 'The temperature in the pool at the hotel where I stay in Madrid is firmly regulated, winter and summer, but here we only need to heat the pool in the winter.'

They paused in the deep end, holding on to the side of the pool. Pippa had to take deep breaths before her breathing steadied and she was able to ask a question.

'Do you still have friends in Madrid?' she asked, her eyes innocently fixed on his face.

Carlos smiled, his face lighting up with animation.

'But of course! Madrid was my home for a long time. In fact, whenever I have to go up there I'm always aware of the number of friends who have invited me to stay with them. Because there are so many it would be difficult to choose. That's why I stay in a hotel, and also it's easier to get on with my work in the evening if I don't have to socialise all the time.'

She knew she was shamelessly probing, but she hoped Carlos hadn't sussed out why.

'Oh, but surely you must spend some evenings relaxing.' She was keeping her tone deliberately light.

'After my work was finished this week, of course I went out into Madrid to meet friends. As you know, in Spain we have dinner very late. Sometimes I got back to my hotel in the early hours of the morning. It was quite tiring, so it's nice to get home and be able to relax.'

She looked at his strong, honest, tantalisingly handsome face and wished she could get rid of the suspicions creeping over her. Why should a man like this remain faithful to someone he barely knew? After one night of impetuous lovemaking why should she expect him to give up the established, privileged life he was accustomed to?

She turned, taking a deep breath. 'Race you back to the shallow end.'

She heard the deep, throaty sound of his boyish laughter as he pursued her. With several strokes he passed her and she was left to follow in his wake, cutting her way through the turbulent water he'd created with his powerful crawl.

Carlos had already hauled himself out of the water when she arrived. He leaned down, putting out his hand to pull her out of the pool. As she emerged, breathless, he pulled her wet body gently against his.

In that moment, as they remained oh, so close to each other, she realised that she didn't mind the thought of him having a busy social life in Madrid. That was OK. It was when her imagination ran away with her and she thought about the woman who lurked in the shadowy part of his life that she minded. How much of a threat was she to his unvoiced plans which Pippa hardly dared to think about?

Carlos returned inside to help Señora Montejo carry lunch down to the pool. A large table was spread with a cloth and Carlos set down the roast chicken, tiny potatoes, green salad and huge mis-shapen Mediterranean tomatoes. He set the large um-brella at an angle so that they were shaded from the rays of the midday sun. Pippa brought Matthew down from the nursery and put him in his car seat beside them, where he seemed happy enough to wait for his feed whilst he listened to the sound of their voices.

Pippa cut sections from a fresh peach and ate as quickly as she could when Matthew's good humour turned to impatience. Retiring from the table, she made herself comfortable on the narrow terrace beside the changing rooms. A couple of days ago she'd vis-ited one of the tourist shops in the village and bought herself an all-purpose sarong which was proving in-valuable now as she covered her bikini. It was more comfortable for Matthew to be cradled against it than her still damp skin.

Carlos was sitting in a wicker chair close by as she fed Matthew. He seemed intent on reading the notes he'd brought with him from Madrid, but occasionally he glanced across at her.

'I plan to report on the conference when I get back tomorrow,' he told her quietly. 'I've got some im-portant ideas to put into practice in the hospital.'

'What was the conference about?' Pippa asked as she shifted Matthew from one breast to the other side.

'Medical staff relations. Basically we dealt with

how to get the best out of our staff. How to listen to what they're trying to tell us when they complain and do something about the underlying reasons for their discontent.'

'I wouldn't have thought you got many complaints from your staff at the San Miguel,' Pippa said quietly. 'Everyone seems to enjoy their job.'

'That's because I keep my ear to the ground and make sure that small grumbles don't escalate into a revolt.'

Pippa felt privileged that Carlos was taking her into his confidence. She smiled across at him. 'I've only got one small suggestion to make about my own working conditions.'

He looked surprised by her bold tone. 'Well then, Staff Nurse Norton, you'd better tell me what your problem is.'

'I'm feeling strong enough to take on full-time work,' she said firmly. 'I know you probably think I should continue to work mornings only for a bit longer, but honestly…'

'Fine! If you feel up to it I'm sure Julia will be more than happy to have you on the ward for longer hours. I'll make the arrangements.'

'Thank you.'

'I'm glad you're enjoying the work. You've settled in extremely well.' He hesitated. 'Have you thought about what you'll do when your contract expires in October?'

'Not really.' She wished her heart would stop pounding so loudly.

'You could always stay on. If you haven't made plans to go back to England I'm sure we could arrange for you to keep your position in the maternity ward.' He smiled. 'Babies are always being born, summer and winter.'

'I'll have to think about it,' she said slowly.

'It's wonderful here in the winter,' Carlos said, his voice husky with animation. 'Very few tourists, the hospital staff are more relaxed, and we have a great time at Christmas.' He paused. 'Yes, think about it, Pippa, and let me know…that is unless you've already made plans for Christmas.'

'I haven't thought so far ahead,' she said carefully.

She'd always known that Christmas was meant for family reunions. But since Matthew was born she'd felt that he was all the family she needed.

Her mother seemed preoccupied with her own life whenever she phoned—apparently her mother and Mike, her second husband, were planning a new life for themselves in Florida. They'd recently bought a small apartment—and were planning to move out there shortly. Her mother had stressed that it was a very small apartment, unsuitable for a baby, she'd said—so Pippa had got the message that she wasn't expected to visit until she was specifically invited. Knowing her mother, that would probably be when Matthew was fully grown! She'd never been keen on small children.

But Pippa was relieved that her mother sounded happier than she had done in a long time. A vision of herself and Matthew still here at Christmas popped suddenly into her mind's eye. She could imagine Carlos carrying a larger Matthew, who would be full of chuckles and smiles…

'So you've no plans beyond October?' Carlos asked quietly.

'Not at the moment.'

Better not to burn her boats entirely! If the worst happened, and it did turn out that Carlos was committed to someone, she would want an escape route. Because, although she loved it out here, she couldn't bear to stay on if the situation changed.

They spent a relaxing afternoon playing with Matthew, who seemed to enjoy being the centre of attention. When the sun began to lower in the sky they went back to the house to have a drink on the terrace.

'You'll stay tonight, won't you, Pippa?'

The question she'd waited for now caught her unprepared. She put down her glass on the small table and looked across at Carlos. Arriving here this morning, she'd planned to say no. But as the day had progressed she'd felt the rapport between them building into a crescendo of mutually warm emotion. His expression as she scanned his face was tender, expectant. She remembered the night they'd spent together. It had only been a week ago but it seemed like a lifetime.

How she'd longed for his return during the days when he'd been away! What purpose would it serve to deny them both another heavenly night together? She would think only of the present. Whoever Carlos may have in his background she didn't want to know—not for tonight anyway.

'Yes, I'd like to stay,' she said quietly.

CHAPTER EIGHT

As Pippa watched the ultrasound screen with her patient she could feel the palpable joy that was emanating from the young Spanish woman at seeing her baby so clearly. Between them they were managing to converse in a mixture of Spanish and English.

In the month that Pippa had been on the full-time staff she'd managed to improve her Spanish considerably, by reading up a little grammar and vocabulary each day and making the most of speaking as much Spanish as she could whenever she was with Spanish people. Carlos was very patient with her, and she'd picked up a great deal in the time they spent together...especially during what could be loosely described as their pillow talk.

She smiled to herself as she thought of the terms of endearment she'd learned from Carlos. You couldn't get that from textbooks! And it was so wonderful to be able to converse with Carlos in his own language at last. It was also good to be able to talk to Señora Montejo during her frequent visits to the house.

Since Carlos had come back from the Madrid conference she'd seen him every day—sometimes in hospital, and always at some point during their off duty. And she'd come to regard the beautiful Fernandez house as a home, the place where she was happier than she'd ever been in her whole life.

Her patient was still exclaiming her own happiness

at seeing the image of her baby on the screen as Pippa slowly manoeuvred the scanner over the patient's slippery abdomen. The hospital was short-staffed in the scanning room, and she had jumped at the chance to help out.

'What's that we can see now, Pippa?'

Pippa smiled. 'That's a little hand, Juanita. I think your baby's waving to you.'

'Can you tell if it's a boy or a girl? No, don't tell me! I prefer it to be a surprise.'

'If you'd really wanted to know we could have arranged further tests, but sometimes it's better to have a surprise—especially with a first baby.'

'Yes, my husband would like it to be a surprise. And it wouldn't be fair if I found out before him. But are you absolutely sure there's only one baby in here?' Juanita patted her tummy and then held up her greasy hand. 'Sorry, Pippa. I've got myself all messy.'

Pippa smiled as she wiped Juanita's hand with a dressing towel. 'There's no doubt at all that you're only expecting one baby. I know you've got twins in your family, but it's not twins—this time!'

Juanita laughed. 'That's a pity! We'd rather hoped to get on with our family as quickly as we can. And having two babies at once saves a lot of time and effort, don't you think?'

'How many babies are you planning?'

'My husband would like six, but I think four or five will be enough.'

'So this little infant on our screen is going to be the eldest of several,' Pippa said, thinking how nice it was to have a happy mother like this, obviously looking forward to having a large, much loved family.

She'd formed the opinion that the foetus was a boy. A scan on this particular machine wasn't actually conclusive on gender, so she was reluctant to make a pronouncement where it was really important to the patient. There were other tests which were more reliable. But when the new, more expensive scanning machine arrived, gender predictions would be accurate.

'Do you like your work here, Pippa?' The pretty dark-haired woman smiled up at her, taking her eyes from the screen for a moment. 'It must be very exciting seeing all these new babies.'

Pippa smiled as she looked down at her patient. 'It's very satisfying. Since we moved the ultrasound scanning room so that it's adjacent to the maternity ward it means that women can get used to the place where they'll be delivered. And it's nice for the staff to be introduced to patients who will be coming in here to have their babies when the time comes. Have you been taken round the maternity ward yet?'

'Not yet. Could you take me round after my scan is finished?'

'I certainly will. You're my last patient of the morning, so if you wouldn't mind waiting a few minutes while I write up my notes I'll show you round and introduce you to some of the staff.'

Juanita was surprised when, during her tour of the nursery, she was introduced to Pippa's baby Matthew, who was propped up in one of the cots, kicking his little legs vigorously and gurgling happily as he watched the mobile suspended above him.

'How old is your baby?'

'Three months,' Pippa said proudly.

'Do you feed him yourself?'

Pippa nodded. 'But I've just started Matthew on mixed feeding to supplement the milk he takes. He likes little spoonfuls of baby cereal, and different tastes of pureed vegetable.'

'Ahh! How lovely! And how convenient to be able to bring him to work with you.'

'It is. The hospital management have been most helpful in that respect.'

'I'm glad you think so,' said a deep familiar voice behind her.

Pippa swung round in surprise and smiled at Carlos. 'You weren't meant to hear that, Doctor.'

'I'm glad I did—if only to hear how your Spanish is improving.'

The patient endorsed this remark. 'Pippa will soon be speaking Spanish like one of us, Carlos.'

'Juanita! How are you?'

'Fine! I'll be much better when I've shed this load!' Juanita patted her tummy. 'Only another three or four weeks, so I'm told.'

Pippa waited while the two of them conversed in rapid Spanish, some of which escaped her, but she gathered that they were old friends. Not surprising. Many of the Spanish patients had grown up knowing the Fernandez family.

She'd finish giving the tour of the maternity ward and then would be technically off duty until this evening. Juanita had now finished chatting to Carlos, so Pippa knew she would soon be free to gather up Matthew and go back to the apartment.

Juanita turned at the door. 'Carlos, Marcos was saying he hasn't seen you for ages. You must come round to see us soon. I'll organise a dinner after the baby is born.'

Carlos smiled. 'I'd like that.' He turned back to look down at Pippa. 'I came to find you,' he said quietly. 'I've got a couple of hours free, so if you haven't any plans, the three of us could go down to the café in the village.'

'Sounds great!' Pippa lifted Matthew from his cot and he started jigging up and down in her arms excitedly.

The café in the village was one of the places where Carlos often took them for a simple lunch. It had become one of Pippa's favourite places to eat. The atmosphere was relaxed and easy. The staff already adored Matthew, and nobody took a blind bit of notice when Pippa breastfed him, with a fork in one hand to scoop up her paella or whatever.

'I've got a jar of that carroty purée that Matthew likes in my bag, so I'll pick it up and meet you in reception, Carlos. Or shall I come back here to…?'

Pippa broke off as she heard the shrilling of Carlos's mobile. She waited as he answered it.

'Maria! Where are you? No! Why didn't you tell me you were coming? Oh, I see… I'd no idea… Yes, of course. I'll come at once…'

As he cut the connection Pippa could feel her spirits plummeting. The worst scenario had happened. The woman she feared most had materialised. For the last month she'd managed to stifle her doubts, but now…

Carlos's expression was troubled as he looked down at her.

'This seems very rude of me, Pippa. Please forgive

me. I'm afraid something important has come up. I won't be able to have lunch with you today, but—'

'It's OK, Carlos,' Pippa broke in quickly. 'You don't have to apologise. I understand.'

She'd rehearsed what she would say so many times, but now she realised that the less she said, the easier it would be for both of them.

'Thank you for being so understanding, Pippa. Perhaps later this evening we could go out for dinner, or…?'

Pippa shook her head. 'Not this evening. I'm on duty, and after that I need an early night.'

She hoisted Matthew on to her hip and began to move away.

'Carlos, can I have a word?' Julia was hurrying into the nursery, fresh and rested from her morning off duty. 'Hi, Pippa, are you going off duty now? See you later.'

'Did I detect a little frostiness in the atmosphere when I burst in upon you and Carlos in the nursery?' Julia asked later that evening. 'I'd only just come on for my afternoon and evening duty so I wanted to catch Carlos before he disappeared for lunch. I hope I didn't interrupt anything.'

Pippa shrugged. She'd spent a miserable afternoon—catching up on domestic chores at the apartment, trying to amuse Matthew, who wasn't sleeping as much during the day now. When she'd come on duty this evening and tried to put him into his cot in the nursery he'd howled lustily and clung to her, until the staff nurse in charge of the nursery had lifted him from his cot and carried him round on her hip while she got on with her work. As Pippa left the nursery she'd had the distinct impression that Matthew had picked up on her anxiety.

Her work on the ward had kept her busy, and her mind had been fully occupied. She'd assisted at a difficult birth and prepared another patient for imminent delivery. But now that her hours of duty were finished the sad restlessness that had enveloped her all afternoon had returned. Julia had invited her into the office for a coffee and, understandably, had asked her what was the matter.

Pippa took a deep breath as she wondered where she should begin and how much she should explain.

'Carlos had just invited me out to lunch when you came into the nursery, and then, after taking a phone call, he cancelled our lunch together.'

Julia sat back in her chair and gave a deep sigh. 'Men! They're all the same. Pick you up, put you down... I'm convinced my Pablo is about to announce he's going back to his wife. He keeps having to spend mysterious weekends in Barcelona, and that's where they have a house.'

'Have they got children?'

Julia's chatter was taking her mind off Pippa's own troubles.

'Of course not! I wouldn't take a man away from his children.' Julia paused. 'And I made sure his marriage was effectively over—or so he said. Sorry, Pippa, I didn't mean that to sound as if I was criticising you. I know that as soon as you found out that Ian was married and had children you ended your affair, didn't you? More coffee?'

Pippa held out her cup. 'Yes, please. I know I shouldn't be drinking this so late, but honestly, Julia,

I doubt whether Matthew and I will sleep much, whatever I drink or don't drink tonight.'

Julia topped up her cup. 'So who was this person who took Carlos away from you at lunchtime? Male or female?'

'Oh, definitely female! Her name is Maria.'

'Ah!'

'What do you mean, ah?'

Julia looked incredibly uncomfortable. 'I'm so sorry, Pippa, but I think you should know something.'

'Know what?'

'Listen, remember when I told you Pablo thought Carlos was involved with a woman from Madrid?'

Pippa nodded mutely.

'Well, after that, I asked him again. And…and he said her name was Maria.' Julia swallowed. 'And the rumours of a relationship were actually about them being engaged. Pippa, I didn't want to tell you, in case…'

'Engaged?' Pippa's voice had reached shrieking proportions. She took it down a few decibels before repeating, 'Carlos and Maria are engaged?'

Julia nodded unhappily. 'That's what Pablo told me. And he's lived around here for years.'

Pippa put a hand to her head. With the other hand she reached down to stroke Matthew in his pram and make soothing noises to let him know he wasn't forgotten. She'd wakened him from a deep slumber to take him from the nursery, and was now wishing she'd left him to sleep on while she had this all important-chat with Julia. Matthew was getting noisily hungry, and she would rather walk down the hill to the peaceful seclusion of her apartment before she started to feed him.

'Julia, I've been such an idiot!'

'No, Pippa, you weren't to know. If anything I should have told you sooner. I didn't want to upset you with rumours from the past, but when you said he'd gone to meet her, that she'd phoned him, I just had to say something...' Julia squeezed her friend's hand. 'We don't really know that there's any truth in them—they're just rumours.'

'There's never any smoke without fire, Julia. You know that.' Pippa laughed bitterly. 'Oh, my God, it's happening to me again. I really loved Carlos. I'd fallen for him just like I fell for Ian. Only this time I thought it was different. But it isn't. I feel so hurt and humiliated.'

She took a deep breath to steady her nerves, steeling herself so that she didn't start crying. 'But I'm going to be wiser this time. I'm going to end it before I get hurt any more. Carlos isn't going to string me along as his mistress...'

There was a light tap on the door, and before either of them could call out Carlos had walked in. The embarrassed silence pointed to the fact that the doctor had been the subject of their discussion.

'I hope I'm not interrupting you, ladies.'

He hovered in the doorway, seemingly uncertain whether his position as medical director entitled him to barge in on two of his staff who were staring at him with hostile expressions.

Matthew chose this moment to start making his presence well and truly felt. His loud pitiful howls had the desired effect on Carlos, who bent down to unstrap him and pick him up, talking soothingly all the while, before making them both comfortable in one of the armchairs.

Looking across at Carlos, holding her now pacified son so expertly on his lap, Pippa felt as if her heart would break. Finding out that he had a fiancée should have killed her love for him, but it hadn't. She still loved him, wanted him, but she was going to harden her heart and stop their affair before she got hurt any more.

But she longed to feel that there had been some mistake. Surely if Carlos was engaged to the mysterious Maria, Señora Montejo wouldn't have welcomed her so warmly into the Fernandez home. The people in the village would have said something... Though she did remember a couple of occasions when the name Maria had been mentioned.

And Carlos hadn't introduced her to his sisters yet. Maybe Señora Montejo didn't approve of Carlos's fiancée and had welcomed Pippa as the opposition. No, this was all wishful thinking, and she wasn't going to get any more involved than she already was. She was going to keep her cool and make a clean break.

Julia put her cup down on the tray and stood up. 'I'll just go and check on the night nurses.'

Carlos put a supportive arm around Matthew as he wriggled on his knee. 'I hoped to find you here, Pippa,' he said carefully, as soon as the door was closed. 'I felt bad about not having lunch with you...'

'That's OK. I had lots to do at the apartment,' Pippa said lightly. 'Let me take Matthew from you.'

'No, he's fine.'

'Well, did you sort out what it was you had to do with this friend of yours?'

'My friend Maria has arrived from Madrid. Teresa, her grandmother, has had a heart attack. I've had to admit her to the cardiac unit. She's in Intensive Care at the moment, and our cardiac consultant will operate as soon as she's fit for surgery. We're all understandably very worried about her.'

'I'm very sorry.' Pippa was truly sorry about Maria's grandmother, but she had to be realistic. The concern Carlos was showing was typical of him. But it only reinforced her theory that he was completely involved with Maria and her family. They were his number one priority and she herself came way down on his list.

She stood up. 'I'm going home now. I'm absolutely whacked and, like I said earlier today, I need an early night.'

She held out her hands towards baby Matthew, but, annoyingly, her son turned away and snuggled up to Carlos. She felt a pang of dismay. All the men in her life were ganging up on her!

'Come on, Matthew. It's time we…'

'Let me at least give you a lift home,' Carlos said, gathering Matthew into his arms as he stood up. 'Of course I'll have to return to the hospital, to be with Maria and Teresa, but…'

'There's really no need. It's not far.'

'I don't like you walking down the hill in the dark.'

'I often do it.'

'Well, let me give you a lift this evening.'

Pippa remained quiet as Carlos drove down the hill to her village apartment. It had seemed easier to give in to his firm insistence that he should drive her. And she was truly glad of being whisked away into the comfort of his car. Her legs were aching from being on her feet all day, and she was planning a long, lazy soak in the ancient half-size hip bath she rarely used because showers were quicker.

Tonight she would indulge herself with every scented bath accessory she could lay her hands on. And she would make plans for a life after Carlos...

'You're very quiet, Pippa.'

'I'm very tired,' she said, in a flat voice. 'These split shifts are more tiring than continuous duty.'

'You don't have to do split shifts. I told you when you took on full-time work that we could make an exception for you.'

'I don't want to be an exception to the rule,' she said quickly.

'I think you should change your mind about that. Perhaps when you sign your new contract...'

'I won't be signing a new contract,' Pippa said quietly.

Carlos drew the car to a halt outside Pippa's apartment and turned to look at her in the half-light of the streetlamp.

'But you gave me the impression that you were going to.'

She drew in her breath. 'I've thought long and hard about this, but I've decided to leave Spain at the end of October and take Matthew to see his father in New York.'

Her fingers were crossed behind her back. She'd never been any good at lying, but this was only a white lie—something to make sure Carlos would accept the fact that she was leaving him.

'But surely...?'

'I think it's important Matthew makes contact with his father while he's still a baby. Seeing you bonding with Matthew has made me realise that a boy needs a father. I think you'll agree with me that family is everything, isn't it?'

She knew she'd touched a nerve when she said this, and she watched the worried expression on his face. She could see that he was torn between his beliefs and his desire to hold on to the wonderful relationship they'd forged between them.

She realised that she knew very little about the rich, privileged background Carlos came from. Maybe there it was accepted that you could have a wife and a mistress. But she couldn't bear to wait around and find out. She'd suffered enough when Ian had tried to have his cake and eat it. Much as she loved Carlos— in a way she'd never loved Ian—she had to say good-bye.

The difference between ending her liaison with Ian and with Carlos was that with Ian she hadn't cared how much he suffered because of what he'd put her through. But with Carlos she couldn't stop loving him. She didn't want him to suffer at all. She wanted him to be happy in his new life—of which she knew she could never be a part.

'Will you stay out there in America?'

She swallowed hard. It was so difficult to lie, but it was the only way she could make Carlos accept that it was over between them.

'I'm not sure. But what I'm trying to say is that I don't think we should see each other again as…as anything more than professional colleagues. I also feel that Matthew is becoming too attached to you, so until I leave it would be better if we didn't meet up except in hospital.'

She raised her eyes to his, and the pain she saw there nearly broke her resolve. But again she hardened her heart, knowing that she herself couldn't bear the kind of pain she'd already gone through with Ian. A clean break was the only way out of this dilemma, so she had to be cruel to be kind—both to herself and to Carlos.

'Are you sure this is what you want?'

'Yes, I'm absolutely sure.'

She opened the car door and put one foot down on the pavement outside. There! She'd made it without bursting into tears, without turning back and snuggling into the comfort of Carlos's arms. She was never going to be anybody's mistress again, with all the hurt and humiliation it involved. She reached over her seat to unstrap Matthew.

'Here, let me do that, Pippa.'

Carlos was already reaching across from the other side, his hands brushing against hers as she struggled to make her trembling fingers work. She was trying desperately to hold back the tears and knew that if she didn't get inside quickly she would make a complete fool of herself.

She turned away, leaving Carlos to extricate Matthew while she fumbled to unlock her door. In the bottom of her bag there just had to be a tissue…ah, there it was…

She dabbed at her eyes before blowing her nose vigorously.

'Thank you, Carlos.' She held out her arms to take Matthew from him.

'Let me carry Matthew inside.'

'No, I can manage.'

'Please, Pippa. We can't just end our wonderful relationship like this!'

Holding Matthew on his hip, Carlos put a comforting hand on Pippa's shoulder. 'Let's go inside,' he said gently.

She glanced across the street to where a young couple had paused to watch them.

'No, Carlos, it has to be this way. And anyway, you've got to get back to the hospital, to Maria and Teresa, haven't you?' She stretched out her arms and took hold of Matthew. 'Goodbye, Carlos.'

As the door closed behind her she clutched Matthew against her, willing herself not to cry until she'd settled him in his cot. She waited until she'd heard Carlos's car going away before she moved along the narrow corridor to Matthew's bedroom.

Matthew was already asleep as she tucked him into his cot, kissing his dear little cheek goodnight.

She straightened up, feeling completely unreal. None of this was happening to her. At any moment she would wake up and find that the dreaded Maria didn't exist. That she was just a figment of her own imagination. Tonight Carlos had seemed exactly the same as he'd always been—except he wasn't. He was Maria's fiancé and that changed everything. Perhaps he'd thought that after he'd married Maria Pippa would be happy to be his mistress. Some women did accept a situation like that. But she knew she never could.

Their affair was over.

CHAPTER NINE

Two weeks had passed since Pippa had ended her affair with Carlos. Two weeks in which she'd found it difficult to sleep at night. She'd lain awake wondering if she was doing the right thing, and then convincing herself that a clean break before she got hurt any more was the only way out. When she left the hospital in October, and didn't come into contact with Carlos anymore, it wouldn't be so hard. Time would eventually ease the pain.

Walking down the hospital corridor now, she could feel her heart beating rapidly. When Julia had told her just now that Carlos wanted to see her in his office, her initial reaction had been to refuse. But then she'd remembered hospital protocol. Carlos was the medical director of this hospital and it might simply be a professional matter he wanted to see her about.

She knocked on his door. A light flashed, telling her to enter. Carlos was seated at his desk. He stood up as she came through the door and moved round the desk to hold out one of the chairs for her. A lock of his dark hair fell over his forehead. He looked so boyish, so desirable, so handsome...

She held her breath as she sat down. The faint scent of his aftershave was disturbing her senses. It was the one he kept in the bathroom where they'd lain together in the huge bath, laughing, flirting, tantalising each other as they sipped champagne before making love.

159

She forced herself to banish the images that appeared in her mind. She just wanted to get through this interview without breaking her resolve.

Carlos went back to the other side of the desk, his eyes boring into her as he leaned across the desk.

'How are you, Pippa?' he asked gently.

'I'm fine! What did you want to see me about?'

'I'm working on the staffing plans for October,' he said quietly. 'So I have to know if you've changed your mind about...'

'I haven't changed my mind,' Pippa said, with a firmness she didn't feel. 'Nothing has changed. I'm leaving here in October, so...'

The door was flung open and a tall, slender woman came in.

Carlos's brow furrowed anxiously. 'Maria, what's the matter?'

'Sorry to interrupt you, Carlos, but it's my grandmother. She keeps asking for you. I've told her you're busy and...'

'I'll come when I'm free, Maria,' Carlos said gently. 'But at the moment—'

'Aren't you going to introduce me, Carlos?'

They were speaking in rapid Spanish, but Pippa knew enough now to understand what was going on. She looked up at the elegant Spanish lady. Her beautiful designer suit was moulded to her perfect figure. She had an attractive face and was smiling down at her with a friendly expression. Even though Pippa had always thought she would dislike this woman, she found herself warming to her. Well, at least Carlos would be happy with a charming wife like this.

Carlos stood up. 'Maria, this is Pippa Norton, one of our staff nurses from England.'

Maria's smile displayed perfectly formed white teeth. 'How do you do, *Señorita*?'

'Muy bien, gracias.'

Maria's smile broadened. 'Such a charming accent. How long will you be staying with us here at the hospital?'

'I go back to England at the end of October.'

'In time for the English winter?'

As Pippa listened to Maria's tinkling laugh she was thinking that at least this well-bred woman had no idea that they had both shared the same man. Would it disturb her if she knew? Carlos was now smiling as he watched the two of them together. What was he thinking? Was he pleased that neither of his women suspected the other of having been a rival?

Maria turned to look at Carlos. 'Carlos, I really must beg that you come to see Teresa at the first possible opportunity. Nobody can settle her like you can, and she's driving me…'

'OK, OK!' he said in a good-natured tone. 'Pippa, would you mind waiting here until…?'

'I think we've finished our discussion, Carlos,' Pippa said evenly. 'I've got to get back to the ward.'

She turned to look at Maria. 'So nice to meet you, *Señorita.*'

As she went to the door she was congratulating herself on a good performance. She could hold out until she was in the corridor before her real emotions kicked in. But there were to be no more tears. Her reservoir of tears had run dry.

The hot month of August had given way to the slightly cooler and more comfortable September weather. Pippa found that walking to and from hospital was becoming easier now that she didn't have to keep stopping to wipe her face with a tissue or take a sip of water from the bottle she always kept in the pram. Even the pram seemed lighter as she went up the hill. And it helped to have Julia with her whenever their duties coincided.

At the beginning of September Julia's boyfriend, Pablo, had unexpectedly left the San Miguel hospital, taken a new position in a hospital in Barcelona and, as Julia had predicted, gone back to his wife. So Julia had moved back into the apartment with Pippa. After a couple of weeks' apartment-sharing Pippa felt that their old relationship hadn't changed much since they were young student nurses together.

'My turn with the pram,' Julia said, as Pippa paused to catch her breath on the hill. 'How you ever managed without me I'll never know.'

'Ah, but I often used to glide up and down in a posh limousine in the old days,' Pippa said, in as light a tone as she could muster.

Julia hesitated. 'It's good you can talk about Carlos. Shows the scars are healing.'

Pippa drew in her breath. If Julia only knew how she lay awake night after night thinking about Carlos, only to fall into a fitful sleep where he figured largely in her dreams. Julia had insisted that Pippa remain in the big bedroom whilst she took the smaller one. So they'd moved Matthew's cot into Pippa's room and Julia had painted over the animals on the walls, replacing them with her own family photographs and pictures.

They'd settled into a comfortable domestic routine together and Pippa found her friend very helpful with Matthew. In fact Matthew, being such a joy to have around, was the saving factor for both of them. Matthew's smiles and laughter, coupled with the warm cuddles he gave both of them, went some way to taking their minds off the absence of the men who'd been so important in their lives.

Julia glanced sideways at her friend. 'You're still not ready to give Carlos the benefit of the doubt, are you?'

Pippa bridled. 'What doubt? Everybody's seen him with Maria. She's always around.'

'Yes, she is.' Julia remained quiet for a while before continuing. 'But they haven't announced that they're engaged or anything.'

Pippa groaned, putting her hand on the pram so that Julia would have to slow down.

'Look, Julia, Carlos introduced me to Maria a couple of weeks ago, when she came into his office. They're always together and I can't deal with that right now.'

She stood still for a moment as the memory of that encounter in his office unnerved her once more. Carlos had been so calm and gentle with her. His eyes, still holding a hint of the tenderness she'd come to love, had been pleading with her to change her mind. She'd really had to harden her heart when she told him nothing had changed.

'You're not over him, are you?' Julia said quietly.

Pippa shook her head wordlessly.

'Well, don't close the door entirely,' Julia said carefully. 'We could be wrong about his relationship with Maria. Although they seem to meet up a lot, they're not exactly lovey-dovey in public, are they?'

'There was a definite bond between them when Maria came into the office,' Pippa said. 'She seems to have some kind of hold over him. I don't dwell on it any more.'

'You mean, you *try* not to think about it. My guess is that Carlos is on your mind all the time…except when you're working, of course.'

'With a tartan of a sister like I've got on the ward, constantly nagging at me,' Pippa said, forcing herself to smile, 'my mind is always firmly on the patients.'

'Hey, don't look now but…talk of the devil!' Julia whispered.

They were passing the entrance to the car park. Carlos's distinctive car had just pulled up and Maria was getting out of the passenger seat. It was more than Pippa could bear. The sight of that well-groomed, stylish lady being escorted to the hospital by the only man she'd ever truly loved…

'I hate to say it, but she's very attractive, isn't she?' Julia whispered. 'Expensive clothes. I'm told she owns a prestigious art gallery in Madrid.'

'Yes, I heard that.'

Pippa took charge of the pram and hurried inside, making her way towards the nursery before Carlos and Maria could see her. Compared to the elegant Maria she felt decidedly dowdy this morning, in her white uniform dress and flat sandals.

After she'd settled Matthew into the nursery she went into Julia's office. She noticed at once that the usually ebullient Julia appeared nervous.

'Sit down for a moment, Pippa,' Julia said in a strange voice.

'What's the matter?'

'Carlos was here just now and… Well, I had a chat with him. I told him the real reason that you're leaving in October is because we've heard he's engaged to Maria.'

'Julia, how could you? You had no right to…'

'I feel responsible for telling you what Pablo told me about Carlos and Maria being engaged. And if it's not true, I'd never forgive myself for having split up such a wonderful relationship.'

'You didn't split us up. All the signs were there—the phone calls from Maria, the way he jumps to do her bidding, the way they seem so close… But, yes, when you told me, my worst fears became reality.' Pippa drew in her breath. 'What did Carlos say when you told him I knew?'

'At first he looked stunned, and then he seemed to recover his composure.'

'But did he admit that he was engaged to Maria?'

'No…not in so many words. He said it was all very complicated.'

'I bet it is!'

'No, listen Pippa. He wants to talk to you about it!'

Pippa shrugged. 'What is there to say, except I'm not willing to play second fiddle to anybody? It's all or nothing with me.'

'I think Carlos knows you won't see him off duty any more, so I'm afraid I've had to arrange that you meet up here in hospital. There's a patient in the delivery suite who's asked for both you and Carlos to be there when she gives birth. She's a good patient. We're well staffed in the delivery suite today, so you and Carlos won't be required to do very much in this early stage. You'll have plenty of time to talk while you're waiting around for the final stages of the birth and, given that you're in hospital, it should be easier than making an assignation away from here.'

'Who's the patient?' Pippa asked guardedly.

'Juanita, one of the patients you've been taking care of. She came in during the early morning. She's asked if she can use the birthing pool, and as you've had experience I thought you might like to be with her. As I said, she actually requested that you be there. I think you've made quite an impression on her.'

Pippa was trying to stay calm and professional, even though her thoughts were in turmoil. 'Juanita is a good patient to deal with. Yes, I'd like to be with her for her delivery. How far on is she?'

'Night Sister says the baby should arrive towards the end of the morning at the present rate of progress. So if you'd like to go along and see what's happening...' Julia hesitated. 'The reason Juanita has asked if Carlos will also be there is because they're old family friends. You may find Carlos is so busy dealing with our patient that he doesn't mention the fact that he knows why you're leaving the hospital, but then again...'

'I wish you hadn't told him. It was all going so—'

'No, it wasn't, Pippa! You were dead miserable. You've got to hear Carlos's side of the story.'

'I'm simply going to do my job this morning,' Pippa said quietly. 'There's no earthly reason why I shouldn't work with Carlos again. We're both professionals.'

'Good girl! I always know I can count on you.'

Pippa smoothed down the front of her uniform dress as she hurried along to the delivery suite. She'd become fond of Juanita and she didn't want to let her down. But the thought of being close to Carlos again after…how many weeks? Three, four…? Yes, it was four weeks since she'd told him she wanted to end their relationship.

She brought herself quickly back to the present situation. Julia had advised her not to close the door on her romance with Carlos. But how could she harbour any hopes when the evidence of his two-timing was so blatantly obvious? She'd even begun to feel sorry for Maria, for the fact that Carlos had been having an affair while his fiancée was away. At least she herself had known the score; Maria probably didn't.

This was all supposing that Maria *was* Carlos's fiancée… No, she mustn't give herself hope. Carlos had said Maria was an old family friend. He'd also told her that their patient, Juanita, was an old family friend by virtue of the fact that he'd known her husband for many years.

But Maria was different. She seemed to hold too prominent a part in his life to be simply another of Carlos's many friends. And whenever she'd seen Carlos with Maria she'd noticed that she treated him with a certain proprietorial manner. Yes, she had come to believe what Pablo had told Julia. Carlos and Maria were engaged to be married. It was only a question of time before everybody knew it.

'*Buenos dias.*' Carlos was standing just inside the delivery suite, looking far too sexy and handsome in a light-coloured suit that moulded against that virile, exciting, muscular body she knew so well.

His eyes held a guarded expression as Pippa joined him.

She could feel her pulses beginning to race again. He always had this effect on her, even in a professional situation like this, when they were simply medical colleagues.

'*Buenos dias,*' Pippa replied demurely, keeping her eyes cast down so that the full effect of his dark, expressive eyes wouldn't reach her and plunge her emotions into even more confusion.

As she began to move away, towards the birthing pool, Carlos put out his hand to detain her.

'I've missed you so much,' he said quietly.

She heard the husky tenderness in his voice and her legs turned to jelly.

'Don't do this to me, Carlos,' she said, turning back and looking up at him. 'I told you when we talked in the office that I'm leaving next month. You and Maria…'

'Maria is simply a friend. Whereas…'

'So you say! But while she's around…'

'Doctor!' A nurse was hurrying over from the pool. 'Juanita is asking for you.'

'I'm coming.' Carlos looked down at Pippa as they hurried over to the birthing pool. 'Later we have to talk, Pippa,' he said, in a quiet firm voice.

'I don't think we've got anything more to say…'

'You're wrong. I've been living a lie and I have to explain it to you. Juanita!'

Carlos knelt down beside the birthing pool to take hold of his patient's hand.

Pippa knelt down beside him, automatically checking the temperature of the water while her heart raced with the impact of his cryptic revelation. What did he mean, he'd been living a lie? Was he going to tell her that he was tired of two-timing Maria and herself, and that he was going to choose between them? Whatever it was, she had to know—and as soon as possible to put herself out of her misery.

She deliberately put the problem out of her mind as she concentrated on her patient and the task of making a safe and comfortable delivery. Carlos was checking on the dilation of Juanita's cervix while she remained relaxing against the side of the pool.

'Not too long now, Juanita,' he said. 'You're a very good patient. I wish all our patients could relax like this.'

Juanita reached out and took hold of Pippa's hand as she crouched at the side of the pool.

'I'm lucky to have my favourite doctor and nurse to help me. And I do so like being in water. I spend hours each day in my swimming pool at home, so it seemed natural for me to give birth to my first child in water.'

'You're a model patient, Juanita,' Carlos said.

'Ahh...!' Juanita pulled a face as a contraction rippled through her abdomen. She squeezed Pippa's hand tightly. 'Oh, dear, I'm just beginning to feel more pain.'

'If you would like me to ease the pain with something...' Carlos began, but Juanita interrupted him.

'No, I want to do this naturally. I know I can. I've done all my exercises and practised often enough. Ah, here comes my husband.'

Pippa noticed how Juanita's face lit up as the tall, distinguished-looking man hurried in through the door.

Carlos held out his hand. 'Marcos, it's good to see you again.'

'And you, Carlos.'

Carlos spoke briefly to his friend, before placing a

low chair beside the pool so that he could stay by his wife's side.

'Sorry I took so long, darling. I've had to make several phone calls while I was outside but everything's organised now. And Carlos tells me you won't have to suffer much longer.'

'I'm not suffering, darling,' Juanita said. 'I'm pretending to be in the pool at home, with the sun shining on my face…'

Marcos reached forward to kiss his wife and the couple remained in close partnership, whispering to each other, oblivious of the medical staff around them.

Carlos took hold of Pippa's arm and drew her to one side, where they couldn't be heard.

'This is how the birth of a baby should be,' he whispered, his voice soft. 'Just the mother and father waiting for their much wanted child. The mother relaxed and calm, enveloped in love.'

Pippa had a sudden mental vision of her own hurried, uncomfortably cramped delivery at the back of an aircraft.

'Definitely preferable to my own delivery,' she said quietly.

'Ah, but you were unique, Pippa, when you gave birth,' he said gently. 'And I feel very privileged to have been there.'

Pippa felt a wave of romantic nostalgia running through her. Why did Carlos have to be so tender towards her? Was he building up her confidence prior to knocking it down when he explained the truth? She had to know what he meant when he said he'd been living a lie.

'I was very fortunate that you were there with me,

Carlos.' Her voice shook with emotion as she spoke. 'You've been very kind to me...'

'No!' His voice was still quiet, but his tone contained a sense of urgency. 'That wasn't simply kindness. I told you that before, and now you've got to hear what I have to say about...about our relationship. I couldn't tell you before, but now...'

'We can't talk here, Carlos. It's too important. We have to go back to Juanita,' Pippa said quickly. 'But I'd like to hear what you have to say.'

'May I come round to your apartment this evening...about eight?'

Pippa nodded whilst her mind skated around the practicalities. Matthew would be asleep. Julia would probably make herself scarce if Pippa explained how important it was for them not to be interrupted. Being such a loyal friend, she might even go out and leave them completely alone.

'Eight o'clock would be convenient,' Pippa said, as they went back to check on Juanita.

Carlos confirmed that Juanita's cervix was sufficiently dilated for delivery, and Pippa checked that their patient was absolutely sure she wanted the baby to be delivered into the water, rather than leaving the pool when the birth was imminent, as some patients preferred. Juanita, now breathing deeply, nodded her assent to a pool delivery.

'Yes, yes,' she said in a strangulated voice. 'I think...I think... Is the baby coming...now...?'

'You can push, Juanita,' Carlos said, leaning over to take hold of the baby's head as it appeared. 'Now, pant...don't push...I'm checking the baby's cord is in the right position...OK, Juanita...a final push... good, good...there we are!'

Pippa felt a sense of relief as Carlos clamped and cut the cord and lifted the baby out of the pool. Even though they had a model, wonderfully co-operative patient, there were always things that could go wrong at the last minute. But here they were with a perfectly formed baby, howling lustily.

'It's a boy!' Carlos told everybody.

Marcos and Juanita were crying tears of happiness, clinging to each other, and Marcos was oblivious to the fact that his expensive shirt and trousers were completely soaked now that he'd decided to join his wife in the pool.

Carlos handed the baby to Juanita for a few moments before Pippa had to take the precious infant away to perform the postnatal checks. Carlos delivered the placenta, then gave a final check before handing the baby back to Juanita, who was now dried off and sitting beside the pool in her towelling robe.

'I'll take you along to your room, Juanita,' Carlos said. 'I need to make some final checks on you.'

Juanita turned to look at Pippa as she was wheeled away, clutching her precious baby boy. 'Thank you, Pippa…and you too, Carlos. The pair of you make a very good team.'

She gave Carlos a knowing look. He smiled, but his expression gave nothing away.

Pippa swallowed hard. Yes, she and Carlos did make a good team—but only in professional situations. Had Juanita, one of Carlos's close friends, been trying to tell her something? Did she know about Maria? Was she signalling that she thought Carlos was making a mistake?

*   *   *

Pippa glanced at the clock. It was almost eight. She'd never felt so nervous.

'Look, sit down and take a few deep breaths,' Julia said, handing her friend a glass of wine. 'Sip that and stop worrying. Matthew is fast asleep now, and I'm going to go out, so you'll have your precious Carlos all to yourself...'

'Julia, he is not my precious Carlos! He's nothing to me any more. He's simply calling in to explain that he's been two-timing both Maria and me and now he has to choose between us. He'll probably say he's chosen Maria because she's been around longer than I have, and...'

'Pippa, this is all conjecture! Wait until you hear what he has to say. Supposing he says that he's going to give Maria the push...?'

'I'll tell him to change his mind about that and hang on to his faithful fiancée,' Pippa said, her tone firming as, with a large gulp, she reached halfway down the glass of wine. 'There's no way I would consort with a man who thinks two-timing is a way of life—a man who is perfectly capable of living a lie and—'

'There's someone at the door, Pippa. It's probably Carlos. I'll let him in and then I'll leave the two of you...'

There was the sound of footsteps along the narrow hall.

'The door was half-open, so I let myself in,' Carlos said as he walked into the room. He looked down at the pair of them, his enigmatic expression giving nothing away.

'I was just going out, Carlos,' Julia said quickly. 'So, if you'll excuse me...'

'Julia, do you have to go?' Carlos said evenly. 'I need to take Pippa to meet someone who can help me explain my situation better than I can by myself. If you could stay and babysit for a few hours…?'

Julia smiled. 'Of course I'll babysit.'

'I can't see why you can't just tell me what you've come to say here and now.' Pippa turned her eyes on Carlos. 'Please, Carlos. Stop being so mysterious. Either you're engaged to Maria or…'

He reached forward and put his arms on her shoulders. She trembled at the renewed physical contact with him, standing absolutely still as wave after nostalgic wave of emotion swept over her.

'Don't do this to me, Carlos,' she whispered. 'Just tell me one way or the other or else go away and don't come back.'

He pulled her against him. 'I'm not engaged to Maria,' he said firmly.

She gazed up into his troubled eyes. 'How do I know you're telling the truth? How do I know you're not going to…?'

'That's why I want you to come with me tonight, to meet Maria's grandmother. She's home from hospital and she will help me to explain the whole complicated situation to you. Please say you'll come, Pippa, because…'

'You've got to go, Pippa,' Julia said forcefully. 'Don't worry about Matthew. I can look after him all night, if necessary.'

Pippa took a deep breath. 'Yes, I'll come with you, Carlos,' she said quietly.

CHAPTER TEN

PIPPA grabbed the knitted shawl she'd recently bought in the village and flung it around her shoulders. It could sometimes be chilly in the evenings. The lime-green cotton frock she was wearing was terribly crumpled, but she wasn't going to waste time changing it.

'Julia, you're sure you can manage? I've got my mobile with me, so you can contact me if you get worried about Matthew or anything.'

'On your way, girl! If I can't manage one small baby for a few hours then I shouldn't be in charge of a whole wardful of the little perishers.'

Pedro sprang out of the car as soon as Pippa and Carlos appeared in her doorway.

'*Buenos noches, Pedro,*' Pippa said.

'*Buenos noches, señorita.*'

Carlos held open the back door for Pippa before climbing into the front beside Pedro. It was almost as if Carlos felt he was still on trial until his explanation had been given. Pippa had ceased to be surprised by anything that happened today and merely sank back against the plush leather seat, closing her eyes and trying to make her mind a blank. All would be revealed later—she hoped!

The car was slowing down. Pippa opened her eyes and saw they were driving up a long drive, illuminated by lamps hidden amongst the lush foliage. At the end of the drive, as the car ground to a halt, she saw an enormous building which looked distinctly like one of the ancient *castillos* where the Spanish aristocracy lived.

So this was the home of Maria's grandmother! Some home! Perhaps it was divided into apartments. No. As she stepped out of the car onto the gravel drive she could tell that this was a private home. There was a certain opulent cohesion about the illuminated windows and the crenellated towers.

But why on earth did Carlos want to bring her here?

Her heart began to beat rapidly as he held out his hand to help her out of the car. She would soon know the answers to her questions.

His expression was solemn. He looked handsome, distinguished in a dignified way. Looking up at him now, she felt that she hardly knew him. What secrets was he harbouring? She couldn't help longing for him to take her in his arms in that impulsive, boyish way she'd come to adore, but he remained motionless as he stood in front of her.

'Come inside, please. I want you to meet Maria's grandmother.'

Pippa's impatience was growing by the second as she followed Carlos along half-lit stone corridors, up a long flight of thickly carpeted stairs, along a huge landing and into a large hall with the dimensions of a ballroom. Down the centre of this dining hall there was a long table, with three place-settings at the very end. Sitting at the head of the table was an old white-haired lady.

Obviously this must be Teresa, Maria's grandmother. Pippa moved forward apprehensively. As if sensing her nervousness, Carlos put his hand under her arm.

The old lady smiled and indicated that she would like Pippa to sit on her left side. Carlos sat down on her right. It was all terribly formal. Pippa glanced across at Carlos and for the first time since they'd arrived he smiled.

Afterwards, Pippa had very little recollection of the meal, because she'd had so little appetite. There had been some kind of clear soup, followed by fish, then chicken, but at that point she'd found it difficult to pretend she was remotely interested in food.

She didn't want food, she wanted information— and reassurance that there had been some kind of mistake. And why they had to come to this domestic castle she had no idea.

The old lady's English was excellent. She told Pippa that she'd spent a year in London when she was young and she liked to read English books. Throughout the meal, she kept the conversation on all things English—asking questions about the theatre in London, the latest plays, the orchestral concerts that were taking place at the Royal Albert Hall or the Royal Festival Hall.

Pippa found herself hard-pressed to answer all her questions, having opted out of cultural activities soon after she became pregnant with Matthew, but she managed to keep the old lady interested in what she had to say about her life in London.

A maid in a black dress and white frilly apron began removing the dessert plates. Pippa felt a certain relief that the meal was over. If someone didn't soon broach the subject uppermost in her mind she would...

'Now, my dear.' The old lady leaned forward and touched Pippa's arm. 'I sense you're impatient to know why you're here.'

Pippa gave her a half-smile. 'Well, it does seem strange…'

'Carlos wasn't sure you would believe him if he told you the true story, so he asked if I would explain it to you.'

Pippa glanced across at Carlos, but his expression gave nothing away.

The old lady ran a hand over her close-cropped white hair. 'The story begins with my love for Carlos's grandfather. Years ago, I was very young and very beautiful…' She paused, her rheumy eyes twinkling. 'Not the old crone you see before you, otherwise the handsome young Juan Fernandez wouldn't have looked twice at me. All the girls were in love with him. He had everything—except money and a position in Spanish society. His family were simple fishermen. My family were…'

The old lady was hesitating, looking at Carlos to help her out with the right words.

'Your family were aristocratic. So your father didn't want you to consort with the likes of the upstart Fernandez family, Teresa.'

Maria's grandmother gave a deep sigh. 'I'm afraid that's how it was, Pippa. Such snobbery in those days was acceptable. Nobody knew otherwise. It broke my heart to be forbidden to see Juan again. But years later…'

Once more the old lady looked at Carlos for help.

'Years later Teresa's granddaughter, Maria, and I became friends and Teresa was always saying how wonderful it would be if we got married.'

'My granddaughter and Juan's grandson,' the old lady said, smiling. 'That would have been my dream come true—and I made sure that Carlos and Maria knew it.'

Carlos leaned forward, his eyes animated in the light thrown from the candelabra on the table.

'Maria and I were good friends when we were children, but even as teenagers we knew we didn't have that spark that would turn into real love. We neither of us wanted to marry each other, but Maria kept up the pretence whenever she saw her grandmother.'

'I wish she hadn't!' the old lady said vehemently. 'Maria should have…how do you say it?…should have come clean before my hopes were raised too high. As it was, she waited until she thought I was going to die, and then got Carlos to come and see me with her to announce that they were to be married.'

'That was four years ago,' Carlos said dryly.

'And Maria is still waiting for me to die.' Teresa gave a chuckle.

'Maria is delighted that you've survived so long, Teresa,' Carlos said quickly. 'During this last scare, when you had another heart attack and Maria came rushing down from Madrid, I made her promise that if you survived she would tell you the truth—that there was no engagement. I said I could no longer go on living a lie and certainly not at the risk of losing the woman I love.'

He leaned across the table towards Pippa, his eyes tender and loving. 'I had no idea you'd heard the rumours and that my deception would come back to haunt me. If only I'd known that was the reason you planned to leave me I…'

'Quite right, my boy!' Teresa said vehemently.

'You should never have agreed to such a plan in the first place. But Maria only did it for the best reasons. She wanted me to die happy. Well, since my operation in your wonderful hospital I've had a new lease of life. I'm afraid I'll probably live to be a hundred.'

Carlos leaned forward to take hold of the old lady's hand. 'I hope you will, Teresa.'

For a moment the old lady looked into Carlos's eyes. 'Ah, you are so like your grandfather in his young days. Be happy, Carlos. I've had a good life, but I still think about what might have been. One shouldn't have to live with regrets.'

She turned to look at Pippa. 'Carlos is a very lucky young man to have found someone like you. I hope when you reach my age you will be still together. Now I'm going to leave you…'

As she moved to stand up Carlos got to his feet and helped her. Slowly they walked to the door together, the old lady leaning heavily on his arm. When they reached the door a maid took over from Carlos, who returned to his seat at the table.

For a few moments neither of them spoke, and then Carlos looked across at Pippa, his eyes alive with tenderness.

'I kept on telling Maria that her grandmother was not as gullible as she thought. And indeed, when Maria told her this evening, on my insistence, Teresa said she was beginning to have her doubts. She'd already suspected that we didn't have a loving relationship. She had the impression that I was in love…but not with her granddaughter.'

'I'm glad I know the full story,' Pippa said carefully. 'It's been hell trying to understand what was going on. Every time I saw Maria with you, always so deep in conversation…'

'Most of the time Maria was worrying about her grandmother, or when she would be able to get back to her art gallery in Madrid. She's flown back there this evening because her grandmother is out of danger now.'

He stood up and came round the table, holding out his arms towards her. 'We've wasted so much time. Do you think we could turn the clock back to those heady days when we saw each other every day and…?'

'I think we might,' she whispered as his arms closed around her.

Pippa lay back against the pillows, watching the dawn creeping over the windowsill. The painful four weeks she'd spent without Carlos had almost been worth it for the pleasure of their ecstatic. reunion. Arriving back here in Carlos's house had been like coming home. And as he'd carried her up to the bedroom she'd felt she would swoon with happiness.

The first time they made love had been feverish and impatient, each of them longing to slake their thirst after the romantic drought they'd endured during their separation. But then, after the briefest of pauses, their passion had reignited in a long, slow rhythm of excitement that had carried Pippa to heavenly heights she'd never dreamt existed.

As she turned to look at Carlos now her heart was so full of love she knew she'd never been so happy in her whole life. As if sensing that Pippa was looking at him, Carlos opened his eyes and gave her a slow, lazy smile as he pulled her into his arms again.

'I don't know how I've got through the past month without you,' he whispered huskily. 'Don't ever leave me again, will you? Have you made a flight booking for next month?'

'Yes, but I was flying to London, not New York.'

'What had you planned to do in London?'

'Work in my old hospital again. I hadn't approached them yet, but they're always short of trained staff,' Pippa said. 'The plan was to drop Matthew off at a nursery, battle through the rainsoaked London streets to the hospital every day, and then back again in the evening to a bedsit. I'm not sure I can bear to give up the idea,' she finished, with a wry smile.

Carlos laughed. 'I must admit it sounds very tempting.' He kissed her gently on the lips. 'But I've got a better idea,' he said as he pulled away and looked down at her, his eyes searching hers to gauge her reaction.

'Will you marry me, Pippa?'

For a few moments, Pippa remained still and silent, mentally pinching herself to make sure she wasn't dreaming. The miracle was happening right now, but it was even more wonderful than she'd ever imagined.

'Yes, I'll marry you, Carlos,' she murmured, before his lips claimed hers once more and they began to make love again.

'We'll have to see if Matthew approves of his new stepfather,' Carlos said, pulling Pippa into the crook of his arm as they lay back against the pillows.

Pippa turned her head sideways to look up at him. 'Oh, there's no doubt about how Matthew feels about you. Sometimes I began to think he preferred you to me. He's missed you this past month, you know.'

'I think we should give him a call and tell him the good news, then,' Carlos said solemnly.

'Good idea. He should be awake by now, and Julia can bring him to the phone.'

Pippa picked up her mobile.

'Pippa! Where are you? Are you OK? Matthew's only just woken so you don't need to worry. I've got him here in my arms. Listen, can you hear him gurgling?'

Pippa laughed. 'Thanks for everything, Julia. I'm here in… I'm with Carlos at his home, and we've got some news.' She glanced at Carlos, who was nodding. 'You'll be the first to know…we're going to get married.'

Shrieks of delight came down the phone before Julia managed to speak again. 'That's wonderful! But how did…?'

'Later—I'll tell you later, Julia. It's a long story. Can you put Matthew on the phone? His new stepdad wants a word.'

The ensuing conversation was so hilarious that Pippa couldn't help laughing at Carlos's attempt to explain what was happening to Matthew, on the other end of the phone. When he finally cut the connection he couldn't stop laughing himself.

'I know Matthew understood that it was something important,' Carlos said, when he finally sobered up. 'He kept changing his sounds and then listening again. And guess what…?'

Pippa waited. 'Can't imagine.'

'I'm sure Matthew said, "Da, da, da…" He knows me already.'

'No, he's supposed to say Mama first. That's my theory.'

'Pippa, I assure you he said, "Dada." Anyway, we won't argue over Matthew. When we have our next baby together—which, incidentally, I don't intend to deliver personally. I'll be in at the conception but then I'll hand you over to an obstetrician. As I say, when our baby is born we'll record his every sound from the first moment until…'

Pippa laughed. 'Until he goes to medical school and or starts dating girls. Whichever comes first…'

'Talking of conception, perhaps we should practise…'

Pippa snuggled against Carlos, feeling raw desire mounting again. 'Do you think it's necessary to practise after the night we've spent together?'

'I believe you have an old English saying? Practise makes perfect? Am I right?'

'Absolutely!' Pippa said, as she gave herself completely to the most wonderful man in the world.

Modern Romance™
...seduction and
passion guaranteed

Tender Romance™
...love affairs that
last a lifetime

Sensual Romance™
...sassy, sexy and
seductive

Blaze™
...sultry days and
steamy nights

Medical Romance™
...medical drama on
the pulse

Historical Romance™
...rich, vivid and
passionate

27 new titles every month.

*With all kinds of Romance for
every kind of mood...*

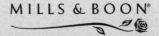

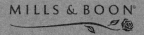

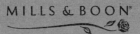

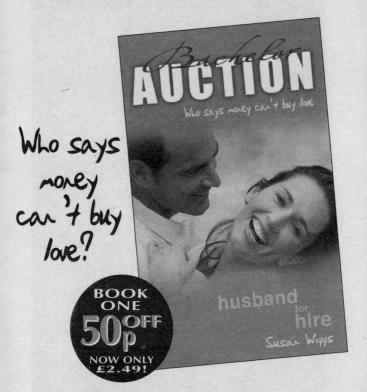

Available from 16th August 2002

*Available at most branches of WH Smith,
Tesco, Martins, Borders, Eason, Sainsbury's
and most good paperback bookshops.*

0802/24/MB47

2 Books
and a surprise gift!

We would like to take this opportunity to thank you for reading this Mills & Boon® book by offering you the chance to take TWO more specially selected titles from the Medical Romance™ series absolutely FREE! We're also making this offer to introduce you to the benefits of the Reader Service™ —

- ★ FREE home delivery
- ★ FREE gifts and competitions
- ★ FREE monthly Newsletter
- ★ Books available before they're in the shops
- ★ Exclusive Reader Service discount

Accepting these FREE books and gift places you under no obligation to buy; you may cancel at any time, even after receiving your free shipment. Simply complete your details below and return the entire page to the address below. **You don't even need a stamp!**

YES! Please send me 2 free Medical Romance books and a surprise gift. I understand that unless you hear from me, I will receive 4 superb new titles every month for just £2.55 each, postage and packing free. I am under no obligation to purchase any books and may cancel my subscription at any time. The free books and gift will be mine to keep in any case.

M2ZEB

Ms/Mrs/Miss/Mr ....Initials...
BLOCK CAPITALS PLEASE

Surname...

Address..

....

....Postcode ....

Send this whole page to:
UK: The Reader Service, FREEPOST CN81, Croydon, CR9 3WZ
EIRE: The Reader Service, PO Box 4546, Kilcock, County Kildare (stamp required)

Offer not valid to current Reader Service subscribers to this series. We reserve the right to refuse an application and applicants must be aged 18 years or over. Only one application per household. Terms and prices subject to change without notice. Offer expires 29th November 2002. As a result of this application, you may receive offers from other carefully selected companies. If you would prefer not to share in this opportunity please write to The Data Manager at the address above.

Mills & Boon® is a registered trademark owned by Harlequin Mills & Boon Limited.
Medical Romance ™ is being used as a trademark.